About the Author

Blanche Dabney is the author of the bestselling Clan MacGregor books, a series of sweet and clean time travel romances set in medieval Scotland.

Growing up in a small village on the west coast of Scotland, Blanche spent many happy childhood hours exploring ancient castles, all the while inventing tall tales of the people who might once have lived there.

After years of wishing she could travel through time to see how accurate her stories were, she decided to do the next best thing, write books about the past.

Her first romance, Highlander's Voyage, came out in 2018, and reader reaction was positive enough for her to dedicate herself full time to writing more.

Since then, she has published more than half a dozen highland adventures, each filled with the passion, danger, and intrigue that are her hallmarks.

Blanche lives in Haworth, home of the Bronte sisters, with her partner and their two children.

instagram.com/blanchedabneyauthor

amazon.com/author/blanchedabney

Also by Blanche Dabney

The Clan MacGregor Series

The Key in the Loch

The Key in the Door

The Key to Her Heart

The Key to Her Past

Medieval Highlander Trilogy

Highlander's Voyage

Highlander's Revenge

Highlander's Battle

Highlander's Time Trilogy

Held by the Highlander

Promised to the Highlander

Outlaw Highlander

PROMISED TO THE HIGHLANDER

A Scottish Time Travel Romance

BLANCHE DABNEY

BLANCHE
DABNEY

TIME TRAVEL ROMANCE

Chapter One

The icy cold Highland breeze hit Kerry Sutherland hard. It blew through the arrow slits as she climbed the last few steps to the tower. She couldn't help feeling that the wind was trying to push her back down to the courtyard.

So many things had tried to stop her from reaching her goal but she wasn't turning back. She'd come too far.

Even if an actual medieval Highlander appeared in front of her with his sword drawn, she'd shove him out the way and keep going. She'd come too far to turn back.

Pausing to catch her breath, she glanced out through the arrow slit. Black clouds were massing over the distant mountains. The peaks had vanished from sight in the time it had taken her to climb from the courtyard. A storm was coming.

She resumed her climb. In a moment she'd be there, standing in the spot she'd dreamed of so often since her childhood, the place where it all began. She held the book tightly in her hand. The Saga of Callum MacCleod. Her closest companion.

Situated at the top of the keep, the east tower soared above the rest of the castle ruins. Somehow it had survived centuries of battle and decay. A single tower that was still complete. At the very top, there was a room that contained the only intact window in the entire place. It had even kept its shutters as if it had been days since they were installed not eight hundred years.

The rest of the keep was a crumbling ruin but somehow the east tower and that window survived intact. Not just intact but pristine, frozen in time while the ravages of countless Scottish winters did for the rest of the building.

The whole tower seemed out of place surrounded by such decay. It looked as if at any moment a burly Scottish Highlander might sweep down from the tower with a stricken maiden in his arms, burst into the courtyard and ride away to freedom and a happy ever after.

Kerry wasn't expecting a happy ever after. She just wanted to see the place where it had begun all those years ago. Her favorite book had spoken of the tower often and finally she was going to see it. All alone and able to imagine herself in the distant past, the Laird Callum himself striding into the room and telling her she would be his bride whether she liked it or not.

There was a lull in the whistling of the wind and for the briefest of moments she heard footsteps right behind her. Someone coming up fast.

She looked back but there was no one there. A trick of the stairs, she told herself. An echo of her own feet rebounding off the stone. That was all it was.

Her cellphone began to ring as she continued her climb. From nowhere an enormous sense of dread crept up on her, making it impossible to breathe. She felt absolutely certain that when she eventually looked down at the screen, his number would be there. He had tracked her down at last.

She knew that was impossible. It couldn't be him. She'd already erased him from her contact list. If only she could erase him from her memory as easily. She told herself it couldn't be him. He was back at home picking his next victim, not chasing after her, not when the police had told him he'd be arrested if he didn't leave her alone for good this time.

Even with that certainty, she didn't want to look down at the screen. She told herself it was because she didn't want to lose her balance on the stairs. The call could wait until she reached the room at the top.

She continued to climb as the ringtone echoed incongruously around the stones. Gripping the rope that served as a banister, she tried to ignore the sound, concentrating on putting one foot in front of the other.

It couldn't be him.

Amazing how he still held her captive, even all this time later. The fear ran deep. She thought back to the relationship ending. It had all been done in such a hurry. Running to her mom's house, shoes in her hand, glancing back the entire time over her shoulder, expecting to find him coming after her.

The blood ran down her forehead, her left eye already swelling shut, making it hard to see anything at all. She ran faster, tears falling down her face. Not this time, she told herself. This time she wasn't going back to him.

Yet, even as the pain in her eye began to spread, she wondered if she was making a mistake. He did love her after all. Was it really his fault that he had a temper? Like he said, she should have known better than to provoke him.

She shook her head. That was him talking, not her. She hadn't provoked him enough to deserve nearly losing an eye. He couldn't love her, not properly. Not with her ear still ringing and her mouth still bleeding.

He'd just ground down her self esteem long enough to make her think no one else would want her, that only he could take care of her. Not anymore, not with an arm that might be broken and an eye that was going to be useless for hours, if not days.

Her run slowed to a walk as she tried to think of what her mom would say to her. In the end she needn't have worried. Her mother had taken her in without a word of complaint, cleaned her injuries, put her to bed in her old room as if she'd never been gone.

That all felt like it had happened a long time ago. The swelling had gone down on her eye though her vision still tended to blur first thing in the morning and last thing at night. The bruises had faded. She was becoming herself again.

It was crazy to think she'd ever considered going back to him, that her mom had to hold onto her while she begged to be allowed to leave, tried to fight to get out of the house and back into his arms when he came round and sobbed through the letterbox yet again.

Sitting in her mother's house, listening to him pleading with her to come out and speak to him, telling her how he couldn't live without her, how it would never happen again if they could only talk for a minute. Sort it all out.

Mom let go of her in the end, told her she had to make a choice. No one could make it for her. She could choose to go be with him, be trapped by her past. Or she could turn and look to her future. She stood with her hand on the front door handle. As he continued to plead with her she froze before letting go of it and running back into her mother's arms, sobbing her heart out as she went

He went away in the end but where he'd gone no one knew. He just vanished. The phone calls to her mom's house stopped. After a month she thought about going back to collect her stuff but she didn't want to risk bumping into him. She knew she wasn't strong enough. It was better to have a fresh start even if that meant having nothing of her own for a while.

Her mom paid for the trip to Scotland for her a month later. "Go get away for a while," she said, handing over the car key. "I'll call you if anything happens. Go have a look at MacCleod castle like you always wanted? Get away from all this and pretend you're Kerry in The Saga."

The next day she was there, in Scotland. When she arrived at MacLeod castle, she headed straight for the tower. Reaching the top of the stairs she emerged into the garret like her heroine had done so all those years ago.

The Saga of Callum MacLeod was her favorite book of all time and she was finally there, where it had actually happened.

She had often dreamed she was the heroine, sharing the name Kerry with Callum's love, being the Kerry in the book, stronger, more powerful than she was, a match for a knight in shining armour like Calum. Or a knight in hose and a tartan baldric. Either way, she wouldn't be complaining.

The bookcase at her mom's house contained a lot of Scottish fiction. While she was recuperating she'd reread many of her old favorites. They were all good reads but only one featured a Kerry. A Kerry who'd stolen the Laird Callum's heart.

Her father had his own theories about the story. He'd even written a paper about it. In her head Callum was always a real hero, leaping from one battle to another and saving damsels in distress, damsels that coincidentally looked a lot like her. For her father, he was nothing more than a Highland fable.

"What do you think happened to Kerry?" she asked him once. "Did she just appear from nowhere like the writer said?"

He smiled at her from his armchair. "You have to remember The Saga was written by a monk who barely knew Callum. It was a story handed down orally no doubt and each teller would have embell-ished the facts. All we really know for sure is that there was a man named Callum MacCleod. Whether he ever met a woman who led to him calling off his wedding?" He shrugged. "Who knows?"

He tried to turn back to his book but Kerry wasn't done. "You must have an opinion, you've got one on everything else."

His frown turned into a smile. "All right, you

want to know what I think? I think maybe there was a Kerry but I doubt it happened like in the story. I think that was only written to make the ending more powerful."

"I don't know. I think he deserves a happy ever after. He went through enough with all those clan wars. I think he deserved to be with the one he loved at the end of it all."

"Even if that wasn't his fiancée?"

"He didn't love her. That was just a marriage his parents arranged for him. He loved Kerry."

"According to the writer. But unless someone comes up with a time machine any time soon, I guess we'll never know what really happened."

Standing in the tower all those years later, Kerry wondered once again. What had really happened? She wanted to continue thinking about Callum but her phone was too distracting.

Accepting the inevitable, she pulled it out and looked down at the screen, wincing as she did so.

She sighed with relief. It wasn't him.

"Hi, Mom," she said, pressing the cell to her ear.

"Kerry, I'm sorry, I'm so sorry."

"Mom? What's happened?" She felt the old familiar anxiety coming back. He'd done something to her mom, she just knew it. Her hand gripped the cell tighter. "What did he do? Did he hurt you?"

"Me? I'm fine, don't worry about me but I couldn't help it, Kerry. He saw."

"Saw what, mom?"

"He turned up yesterday at the house and I was expecting a parcel so I'd already opened the door before I knew it was him."

"Mom? What did he see?"

"The brochure for the castle. He'd picked it up out of the recycling. He asked if you were there. Started ranting about the book, how you were obsessed with that piece of...well he wouldn't stop swearing."

"Did you tell him I'm here?"

"No, love. I told him I was calling the police as that was theft going through my bins like that and he left." She paused for a moment to compose herself. "Please be careful up there. I don't know where he went."

Kerry's blood ran cold. What if he was coming for her? Footsteps echoed up from the staircase behind her. She shook her head. It couldn't be him. He couldn't have made it so far so quickly. He would have had to drive all night and even then how would he know she was at the castle?

Mom's car, she suddenly thought. She'd borrowed Mom's car. What if he'd seen it in the parking lot outside? She was suddenly certain it was him coming up the stairs.

"I've got to go," she whispered, hanging up the cellphone and trying to think clearly. The footsteps grew louder.

It can't be him, she told herself. It was just a tourist wandering around the castle like her. He wouldn't come this far just to get to her. It was over. She'd told him, her mother had told him, even the police had told him. It was over and he had to stay away from her.

She looked for somewhere to hide. There was nowhere. Just four walls and a window. She leaned out. A sheer drop down to the grassy bank of the dried up moat at least forty feet below. No ledge to cling onto. Nothing.

She turned back to face the staircase. There was no time to do anything else.

A hand appeared in the doorway and then a man emerged from the darkness, stepping into the room. The man she wanted to see least in the world.

"Hello, Kerry. Enjoying your vacation?"

"What are you doing here, Edward?" she asked,

backing slowly away from him until she reached the window.

He looked happy but his smile didn't touch his eyes. They were filled with darkness. He was going to hurt her again. She wished her hands would stop trembling.

"Did you think I'd forgotten about The Saga of Callum MacLeod? You banged on about it often enough. Your favorite book, remember? Godawful and clearly written by a talentless moron. Kerry the fair maiden and her Highlander hero.

"I could never compete with him, could I? I was only real and here while he was dead and buried eight hundred years ago. Why wouldn't you want him over me?"

"Are you jealous of a character in a book?" She kicked herself. Don't give him anything. He'll only use it as ammunition.

"I'm not jealous of anyone." He stood blocking the doorway. "You know you stabbed me in my heart when you left? How could you do that to me? Why would you hurt me like that?"

"Don't," she said, shaking her head, trying to control her racing heart.

"Don't what? Don't tell my partner how much

she hurt me when she ran out of my life? It's time to go home, Kerry. With me."

"I'm not your partner anymore, Edward."

"Yes -," he yelled before gaining control of his temper, "- you are. You don't get to just walk away like this. After everything I've done for you, how could you? You made me look a fool at the golf club. I had to cancel the engagement party. Lost the deposit as well. I suppose you're happy about that too?"

"You hurt me," she said quietly, unable to look him in the eye. She cursed herself. Kerry in The Saga would be brave enough to look her enemies in the eye.

He took a step toward her. "You hurt me more. You know I hate having to punish you. If you'd just do as you were told, it wouldn't have to be like that."

"Leave me alone, Edward."

"It's time to come home, Kerry. Put all this behind us."

"I'm not going anywhere with you."

"Yes you are." The words were a distraction. He pounced as he spoke, his arms outstretched, reaching straight for her neck. He always went for her neck first.

She shrieked, leaning back away from him, forgetting she was in front of the window. Her legs tipped back over the sill and then with a sickening lurch in her stomach she fell out of the tower.

For a brief moment time stood still and she could see his arms stretching toward her, almost touching but not quite. Then the moment passed and she began to plummet down to earth, the tower walls rushing past, the ground coming up far too fast. There was the sound of wind whistling past, then a thud, and then it all went black.

When she opened her eyes she had no idea what was happening. All she knew was she was laid on her back with a splitting headache and two women in wimples looking down at her.

"Praise the Lord," one said in a broad Scottish accent, touching Kerry on the forehead as she did so. "She lives."

She tried to sit up but she couldn't manage it. Behind the women she could see a castle tower. There was something familiar about it but she couldn't place it.

A jolt to her memory. A castle. She'd been on a trip to a castle recently. It couldn't be the same one of course. The one she'd visited was ruined and broken apart from one tower. This place looked brand new. It had flags flying, a slate tile roof covering the keep, guards on the battlements, white-wash on the walls.

"Call for the apothecary," the older of the two women said to her colleague who ran off at once. "Are you still with us, lass?"

She tried to answer but the heavy veil was descending again. A second later all was darkness.

Chapter Two

Callum MacCleod swung his sword to the right, slicing into his opponent's arm as if it were butter.

The man went down looking shocked. He had Callum's men outnumbered three to one yet Callum had managed to deal him a fatal blow.

Callum didn't pause. He saw a shadow in the corner of his eye. With a roar he turned, raising his shield just in time to fend off the counterattack. He could tell the battle was already won even if they couldn't. The MacDonalds were fighting to the end but they were doomed.

Callum's men encircled the remaining few aggressors. As soon as the MacDonald warriors realized they'd lost they should have run. Callum would not have chased them. He was content to let them go back home and warn the others what happened to raiding parties caught sneaking onto MacCleod land to try and steal grain.

The remaining half dozen were too stubborn, refusing to give up even though they no longer had any chance of success.

It showed the difference between the two clans. MacCleods knew when to cut their losses. They also had better technique. They trained hard every single day after turning ten. The MacDonalds did not.

Callum yelled above the sound of swords slamming into shields. "Throw down your weapons and walk away with your lives."

There was no response other than ever more frantic sword swinging from the MacDonalds.

"Suit yourself," Callum said quietly, raising his blade above his head. As he did so, he heard an unexpected cry behind him.

He turned in time to see something he never expected to see. Someone had thrown a dirk at Orm. That was where the scream had come from. The knife struck Orm in the chest and he was already falling to the ground.

One of the MacDonalds saw his opportunity

and thrust his blade forward. Orm was skewered on the end of a MacDonald sword, swinging his own at the same time, bringing down his attacker with the last of his strength. The two men collapsed to the ground together.

Callum saw red. One of his oldest companions, Orm had been by his side for almost two decades. Felled by a MacDonald and not even in war, just by a stupid raiding party chancing their arm on the grain store nearby.

Callum ran at the few remaining MacDonalds in a rage. They took one look at him and turned, sprinting up the glen like whipped horses. Callum's roar was still echoing around the glen as the last of them vanished from sight over the peak.

"Should we go after them?" Ross asked, wiping sweat from his brow.

"Nay," Callum replied, getting his temper back under control with some effort. "Could be a trap. Keep a sharp eye out though."

His sword dripped blood as he turned to kneel beside Orm.

"To the devil with them," Orm said with a grimace, prodding the dead man beside him. "I let my guard down. My own fault."

Callum managed a smile. "And I dinnae recall giving you permission to go to our ancestors yet. On your feet, laddie."

Orm coughed up blood that ran down his chin in a trickle. "I regret I cannae obey you, my Laird." His hand clawed up at Callum, his skin turning pale. "I dinnae want to die out here so far from my wife."

"I know."

"Tell Moira I love her, won't you."

"Aye, I will that."

Orm's eyes remained open but the spark in them faded with the last of his words.

He was gone.

Callum wasted no time. He stood up and faced his men. "We bring him back to Frazer castle with us."

None of them argued. The body would slow them down but not one man suggested leaving him behind.

Callum hefted the body onto his shoulders and then made his way through the glen to where his horse waited beside the others. Loading Orm onto the beast's back, he then walked beside it as tradition dictated. It would be the last journey Orm took, he was duty bound to ride it alone. As the man in charge of the patrol, Callum walked.

The group headed back to the track they'd been following when they were ambushed. The MacDonalds were getting desperate. That could be the only reason for such a foolish assault. He had heard rumors their harvest had been poor enough to send them raiding but the bad weather affected all the Laird. He didn't take his men on raiding parties into the land of rival clans. He tightened his belt and ate less so that what stores they had would last the winter.

Rumor had it the MacDonald feasts were as large as ever despite the approaching winter. They were being led by a fool and men were dead because of it. Men like Orm.

He shook his head at the senseless waste of life. The dead men would have been better utilized in the fields than in skirmishes. Now there were two dozen fewer MacDonalds to bring in the harvest. It was foolish logic the MacDonalds employed in their efforts to keep their people fed. Old Malcolm MacDonald would probably shrug when he heard and declare two dozen fewer mouths to feed was always the plan. He was the biggest fool of the Highlands and Isles.

Callum's thoughts turned to Orm. Deaths were not uncommon during patrols, that was always the risk you took protecting the clan. Somehow he had never thought Orm would be one of the fallen. He had seemed invincible, even when they were children. A wooden sword blow that would fell most would just have Orm laughing and spitting in the dirt with derision.

"Remember when he shoved Tommy into the pig swill?" Ivar asked. "I nearly wept, it was so funny."

Callum managed a smile. He well remembered their old sword master coughing out bits of turnip peel and wondering how he'd been bested by a ten year old who was half his size.

"Or when he jumped into the moat to avoid his lessons."

"Aye, couldn't swim and would rather drown than mark a slate with his name."

"What about when he found out Moira was pregnant? Never saw him so happy."

More memories followed, the men laughing as they recalled all that Orm had done with his life.

Callum remained silent. What hurt him most was the way it had happened. It wasn't a noble war to push the Normans out or get the Northmen back to their ships. It was a foolish wee ambush by the weakest clan in the Highlands and Isles. Not just that but a knife to the chest and all because Callum didn't check one of them was dead.

"It's not your fault," Hamish said from the back of the group of riders.

"Och, dinnae do that," Callum replied. Hamish had an unnerving habit of being able to read his thoughts. "It's not your place to say who's to blame."

"I tell you something," Ewan said. "He should have stopped patrolling when he wed his wee lassie. He let his training slip once he was married. Got fat."

A murmur of agreement from the other men. Callum turned from one face to the next, feeling a hint of mutiny rising.

"He was bound by his oath to protect the clan," Callum said. He couldn't admit it but he agreed with his men on the matter. It was one thing to swear the oath but to continue patrolling once wed and with a pregnant wife waiting back at home?

"Moira begged him to stay," Hamish said. "He told her nothing would happen. 'I'll be back soon enough. We'll go to MacLeod castle together when I return and stake out that farm together like I promised.' No lass could manage that land alone. Such a waste. Married men should stay at home."

Another grumble of agreement.

Callum looked at Orm's body on the back of the horse. He thought about how Moira would take the news. A tiny part of him wanted to give the task to one of his men but he couldn't do it. It was his job as Laird's son just as it was his job to walk so Orm had one final horseback ride through their land.

"Married men should not patrol," Ross echoed, bringing him out of his reverie.

"Better that men who patrol do not wed," Callum replied, bringing grunts of agreement from the others. "Orm was told but he wouldnae listen. Spoke of love like that mattered more than protecting our people. Now I must inform a widow with bairn on the way that her man is dead. The oath is no small thing. It does not fit well with marriage."

"What will you be telling your bride to be then?" Hamish asked, looking pointedly at him.

Callum winced. "Dinnae remind me of that. I tell you what I told my father. I will never wed."

"I'd like to be there when you tell the Laird you're turning down his choice of bride."

Callum wasn't looking forward to talking to his father again. He had told him before that he had no intention of ever marrying but that was before the wedding had been arranged. He had managed to put off the conversation before this patrol but she was already on her way from the mainland. Time was running out for him to get the matter dealt with before she turned up and started getting measured for a wedding dress.

They reached Frazer castle at noon on the second day. Callum left his horse outside and entered alone. "Have you seen Moira?" he asked the first person he encountered, a wee slip of a lassie who was struggling across the courtyard with a heavy tray of fresh smelling oatcakes.

"Aye, in the great hall with the others. I'm to fetch these in for them."

"I'll take them for you."

"You're a noble. You can't-"

He interrupted. "You can barely move for the weight of them. How old are you? Twelve?"

"Ten, my Laird."

"I'm not the Laird. I'm just his son."

"Just a Laird's son taking a tray of oatcakes from a kitchen skivvy." She giggled as he lifted the tray from her arms.

"Here," he said, tossing her an oatcake. "You look like you need it."

He crossed the courtyard, taking the stairs up to the keep two at a time. Ducking his head to enter, he stepped straight through the open doorway into the huge room beyond.

Inside it was heaving with people. He took in the scene quickly. There were petitioners lined up at one side, warming themselves by the fire. His heart sank as he realized there could only be one reason why so many people were waiting to be seen. His parents must have traveled from MacCleod castle and if that were the case, he doubted it was to visit the Frazer family. They'd come looking for him.

"Callum," a voice called out from the far end. "My son, what are you doing back here? I was told you were patrolling for another week."

"I was, father," Callum replied, passing through the crowd so he could reach his parents who were sitting together on the dais.

"Perhaps you might tell us why you have returned so soon, covered in blood, and carrying oatcakes like a serving girl. Were you so hungry you laid siege upon the kitchen."

A laugh went up among the petitioners.

"We were attacked."

Silence fell upon the crowd. They all feared that war might return. It had been little over a year since William had bought his crown back from Richard of England and many thought Richard was sure to double cross the Scots sooner or later, bring his armies back north, perhaps as far as the islands. The truce held but only just.

"Attacked by whom?" the Laird asked, sitting upright on his throne. "The bastard King Richard?"

"MacDonald men."

"MacDonald?" He spat into the dirt, arms folding across his chest. "Lose anyone?"

Callum nodded. This wasn't how he wanted the conversation to go. He wanted to speak to Moira on her own. He looked around, spotting her over in the corner, sitting with her ladies in waiting, dress barely concealing the swelling of her belly. Callum felt an immense wave of sadness wash over him. The bairn would never know its father, only hear tales of what a noble warrior he'd been.

"What happened?"

"They ambushed us at the fairy glen."

"Heading for the grain store no doubt," his father said with a nod. "Did you leave any alive?"

"Aye, father. Half a dozen."

"Why? Why not kill them all."

"They're hungry like us. What good would it have done to slaughter them?"

His mother looked at him, seeing his face and understanding at once. "Hold a moment, Alan. Callum, who did you lose?"

Callum paused for a brief moment. Moira was not looking at him. She was looking at the children playing nine men's morris on the floor in front of her, smiling as she pressed a hand to her bump. He was about to ruin her life and he desperately wanted to give her a few precious seconds before he did it.

"Well?" his father asked. "Who died? Spit it out boy." The room waited. Even Moira looked across at him.

"Orm."

A scream from behind him. Moira fell to her knees, sobbing wretchedly, thumping the rushes with her fists. "My Orm!"

"A good man," the Laird said quietly, stroking his chin. "May he rest in peace."

Callum watched as the ladies in waiting led the weeping Moira away. She turned as she went, glaring at Callum for a moment. He did not shy from it, taking her rage before she vanished out of the end of the room.

"Tell me exactly what happened," the Laird said when she was gone.

Callum told him everything. When he was done, the Laird nodded. "Gillian, my love. Write a letter to Malcolm demanding parley. This cannot go on. We will have no stores left and he'll have no men to raise armies when the English come."

"And if he doesn't listen?" Gillian asked him.

"I will make him, my dear." He clapped his hands together and managed a smile. "Though it is under a cloud, I am glad to see you, my boy. I have some news about your bride to be."

Callum knew exactly what he was about to say. "I have no wish to marry, father."

"Now dinnae start that again. She is on her way to MacLeod castle and you will go there at once to await her arrival. Is that understood? No more sneaking out on patrol to avoid the inevitable."

"Do you no ken, father? I dinnae want no lassie to shriek over my death like Moira over Orm. I'm a warrior, not a family man. I wouldnae even ken what to do with bairns if they were put on my knee."

"This isnae about you, Callum. Maids raise

bairns. You just do your duty to keep the clan line alive. Our alliance with the MacKays depends upon this wedding."

"My duty is to protect our people and I failed at that. I want to bury Orm, not put a ring on yon lassie's finger."

"Enough!" The Laird got to his feet. The entire room had fallen silent. That never happened. He never shouted.

Slowly, he resumed his seat, his voice returning to normal. "You will go and you will be there when she arrives. So put your bloody oatcakes down and get moving before I shove my sword down your throat. I will take care of Orm's burial. You go meet your bride to be and by thunder you better be good to her. There's a lot riding on this, my boy. I cannae fight the Normans, the Northmen, the MacDonalds, and the MacKays all at once."

He put the tray down on the table beside him. As he did so his mother squeezed his hand. "You might like her," she said. "Give her a chance."

He managed a curt nod. "I better be going, mother."

She let go of his hand, smiling warmly. "Give her a chance."

His men were waiting outside, Orm's body laid

out on the back of a cart next to them, tartan cloth draped over him. "I must go back to MacCleod castle," he told them. "The Laird will help you bury Orm. If you see Moira, tell her...just tell her she will want for nothing. The clan will see to that. And tell her I'm sorry."

He walked away, heading out of the castle to untie his horse from the hitching post. Climbing onto its back, he rode slowly north, a heavy ball in the pit of his stomach like he'd swallowed a lump of molten slag from the smithy pit.

Marry a woman he'd never met to cement an alliance between two feuding clans? It happened all the time in the Highlands but that was to other people. He was different. He wanted to remain single. He didn't want to burden anyone with worry over what might happen to him whenever he went on patrol.

What he needed was to think of some way to get rid of her that would not infuriate his father or the MacKays. He couldn't just refuse to wed. Do that and he would be cast out of the clan, shunned by his own kin, a fate far worse than marriage.

Perhaps he could persuade her to back out of the wedding. The thought comforted him as he tried to work out how that might be possible.

Soon Frazer castle was far behind him but he barely noticed, he was too busy thinking. He had a day and a night until he reached MacLeod castle. Little did he know it but the tale that would become The Saga of Callum MacCleod had just begun.

Chapter Three

Kerry opened her eyes to find a Highlander staring down at her. He looked a lot like the man from her childhood dreams, the man who'd come on horseback night after night to rescue her from dragons or cruel lords or from being locked away in some tower or other. Was this a dream too? Was she still asleep?

"Hello," she managed to say, blinking away the blurring of her vision, her throat too dry to add anything to that first word. It couldn't be a dream. Her throat hurt too much.

"I willnae marry you," the Highlander said, folding his arms as he did so.

"Sorry?" Kerry replied, coughing as she tried to

sit up. Shuffling her arms up the bed, she managed to get half upright, taking a better look at the man staring back at her.

He was tall and broad, bare chested apart from a tartan baldric across his chest. He looked a lot like one of the illustrations in The Saga of Callum MacCleod. No wonder she'd thought it was a dream.

His hair was dark and close cropped though the ends were a mess, as if cut by knife rather than scissors. His eyes blazed as he stared at her. She felt as if she'd clearly done something to infuriate him though she had no idea what.

Even angry he looked good, strong cheekbones, chest muscles she could ski off, legs almost splitting the hose that struggled to confine them. He was tall and broad shouldered, filling the room so much she was surprised the walls weren't bulging outward to accommodate him.

"You're a fine looking lass," he continued. "But it wouldnae be right. I cannae see you get left behind and hurt by me dying in battle. I will not have you weep like Moira for Orm. Get well and then get yourself home. I willnae marry you."

Kerry coughed again. "That's good to know,"

she said. "If it helps, I wasn't planning on marrying you either."

"Dinnae mock me. I dinnae take kindly to jests."

"I'm not mocking you. I swear, right now marriage is the last thing on my mind. Maybe buy me a drink first? Or start by asking me my name perhaps?"

He scowled at her attempt at humor, walking away without another word.

The door closed and then she was alone. She sat up further, looking around the room, trying to remember how she'd got there.

The last thing she remembered was being on the phone to her mom and then something had happened. What was it?

The room itself was like something from a movie. She felt as if she'd wandered behind the velvet rope in a National Trust property somewhere, sneaking into a bed she was most definitely not supposed to touch. It was clearly hundreds of years old and yet it wasn't at the same time. It looked new but that wasn't possible.

She ran her hands over it, feeling the coldness of the surface. It was made of wood and solid enough. Tartan wool blankets covered her, the same color and style of tartan the strange man had been wearing across his chest.

The walls were white plaster and covered in tapestries. Instead of light fittings there were candles attached to the wall in iron stands. A single window to her left was open but there was no glass in it and the sill was at least two feet broad, set in thick walls. Beyond the window was bright light but from her position all she could see was a pale blue sky outside.

The floor was covered in straw and smelled sweet, like being in a barn just after harvest. There was not a single modern thing in the room. Apart from her.

Where was she? How had she got there?

The door at the far end opened and a woman in a wimple walked in, the rushes shifting under the hem of her white linen dress as she crossed to the bed. She was carrying a tray in her arms. "You're awake," the woman said. "And I see you've already annoyed Callum."

"Callum?" Kerry blinked, wondering if this was a dream. "You don't mean Callum MacLeod, do you?" His face came into her head again, her body stirring as she thought how good he'd looked despite his anger.

"Aye, lass. Are you saying your fiancé didnae introduce himself properly before he stormed off?"

"My fiancé?"

"Aye. You really did do some damage to your head if you dinnae remember getting engaged to the Laird's son. Here, drink this." She set the tray down on the end of the bed and passed a horn cup over.

"What's in it?"

"Nettle tea. Good for after a fall."

Kerry took a sip. It wasn't as bad as she'd been expecting. "You should try adding mint sometime. Is that what happened to me?" she asked as the woman straightened the blankets. "Did I fall?"

"Aye lass. We got a couple of the blacksmith's boys to carry you up here."

"And where is here?"

"The tower room."

"The tower room of…?"

"MacCleod castle of course."

Kerry felt her head pound as she tried to take it all in. "You're telling me I'm in the garret of the east tower of MacCleod castle and I'm betrothed to Callum MacCleod?"

"Aye, lass. I'm glad your memory is returning, is it not? You know about this place then?"

"Sort of. I read it in a book. Can you help me up?"

"I'm not sure I should. I'm under strict instructions to keep you resting for at least a week."

"Either help me up or I'm doing it anyway." She swung her legs out of the blankets, surprised to see they were uncovered. "Where are my clothes?"

"You were naked when you were found, lass. We wanted to wait until you woke to dress you." Her voice dropped to a whisper. "Was it bandits?"

"Was what bandits?" Kerry snapped, wrapping the blanket around her as she got slowly to her feet, the woman holding her arm to help.

"That stripped you and left you for dead outside the walls. We heard nothing but then you were just there. Did you fall from a horse or something?"

"Who's we?"

"Me and Melissa. We were gathering the last of the blackberries when we found you. Not much point, they're long past their best but they do still make good dye, I suppose. Do you really not remember any of this?"

Kerry almost stumbled as pain wracked her skull. A question had to be asked but she didn't want to know the answer, not really. "If this is the tower and that was Callum MacCleod, what year is it?"

"It's the year of our Lord, 1190, October the fifteenth to be exact."

"1190?"

"Aye."

"As in the year 1190?"

The woman nodded.

Kerry crossed to the window and looked down. Far below she could see a raised earthwork above a moat, thick brambles coating the slopes, sheep on top pulling at tufts of yellowing grass.

Lifting her head she looked out at the countryside beyond. It was a sea of greens and browns, low hills that rose past woodland to distant mountains. To the left, just visible, the ocean sparkled and shimmered like sunlight on a mackerel's back. No roads, no cars, no houses. Just fields and mountains and the ocean beyond.

"This isn't a dream, is it?" she asked, turning back around to face the woman. "This is real, isn't it?"

"As real as I am," the woman replied, holding out a linen nightshirt. "Now come and get back into bed before you faint."

Kerry let the woman dress her before guiding

her under the blankets once more. She'd seen Back to the Future enough times to know what was happening though arriving in the past naked had more of a Terminator vibe to it.

She was in the middle ages. Stephen Hawking eat your heart out. She couldn't tell anyone how she'd done it though if she ever got home again. She had no idea how it had happened. She couldn't remember anything between talking to her mom on the phone and then waking up to find that Highlander telling her he wouldn't marry her.

That reminded her. Why did they think she was his fiancée? Who had they mistaken her for? And more importantly, what would happen if his actual fiancé turned up? "Do you know my name?" she asked the woman who was busy pouring more nettle tea into the horn cup.

"Aye. Of course I do."

"Who am I?"

"You're Nessa MacKay. Are you all right? You look awful pale all of a sudden."

"Could you let me rest a while. I feel a little queasy."

"Of course. I'll go fetch some lamb's mint. It's good for the stomach."

She left, closing the door behind her. Kerry sank

into the bed, pulling the covers up to her chin. "Relax," she told herself out loud. "Just relax. There's no need to panic. What would Marty McFly do? Probably try and get off with his mom, that's not much use to me. What about the Terminator?" A thought occurred to her. "Maybe it's more like Quantum Leap. Maybe I'm here to change something about the future. Ah, but Doc told Marty never to change the future. Which is it?"

She pulled the blanket over her head, shutting out the world above as she worked out what to do next. "One thing for sure, I can't do much until my memory comes back. If I'm here to change things, I better wait and see what pops up. What else can I do but wait? I sure can't get home until I work out how I got here."

With a decision reached, she let her head emerge from the blankets again. The pain in her skull ebbed away, as if it had been waiting for her to choose to accept the reality of where she was.

"I'm in the past," she said, smiling broadly. "I get to see what it was actually like then." Her smile faded as she thought of her father. He would have killed to have been in her position. She felt a wave of sadness as she realized that even if she did make it home, she'd never be able to discuss it with him.

He was dead. That was something she remembered. He was a medieval history professor and he'd died of cancer four years ago. Well, four years ago and eight hundred years in the future. He hadn't even been born yet. That thought made her head hurt again. What about her mother? She had just spoken to her before this happened. What had they been talking about?

Nothing else came back to her before the woman reappeared holding a bunch of strong smelling mint. "Nibble on this," she said, passing it to Kerry. "One leaf at a time."

"What's your name?" Kerry asked. "You didn't say before."

"I'm Sheena. Are you hungry yet? Dinner is not for another couple of hours but I could have the kitchen prepare something cold for you if you like?"

"I would love that, thank you."

"I'll go tell them at once."

"Can I come with you?"

"Do you feel strong enough?"

"I think so."

"Then I shall fetch some proper clothing for you. I'll be right back."

She returned a few minutes later bearing an armful of things. "You might have to help me dress," Kerry said, not sure what part belonged to which. "What are these things?"

"This is a kirtle," Sheena said, dropping something a lot like the nightshirt over her head. "Do you really not know that?"

"I've forgotten a lot," Kerry covered. "Would you mind telling me what this lot is?" She put her arms up for the dress to go over the kirtle.

"The girdle helps bunch it up," Sheena said, wrapping a thin woolen belt around her waist. "The fashion at the moment is for lots of folds. Try it this way. That's it. Now put the hose on."

Her legs were clad in plain hose and then she was provided with loose fitting leather shoes, seams on the outside.

"What's that?" Kerry asked as Sheena picked up the last item, a white linen box.

"Your hat or do you want the world to see your hair and think you're available? Only young lassies looking for a man have their hair on show around here."

Into the hat, Sheena shoved most of her hair before passing her a pair of detachable sleeves that buttoned onto the dress. They hung down low from her arms and Sheena shook her head as she looked at them.

"The latest fashion," she said by way of explanation. "I'm not a fan, myself but then I'm out of
touch about most of the newfangled stuff that
comes from Europe. How does all that feel?"

"Heavy and hot," Kerry said before apologiz-
ing. "Sorry, I don't mean to sound ungrateful. It
looks lovely."

"You're only hot because of the fire in here.
Wait until you get out into the wind outside. One
thing though, we better avoid Callum. He doesnae
want you wandering the castle."

"Why not?"

Sheena looked torn, as if trying to decide what
to say. "He doesnae want to see you."

"He said that?"

"Aye, I saw him while I was getting your dress.
Said you're not to speak to him and he'll not speak
to you. When you're well, he wants you to go home
at once."

"And where is my home?"

"Why, back on the mainland of course. Are you
sure you're well enough to go walking? Your
memory is as patchy as my sewing skills."

"I think the fresh air will do me good."

"You'll not get much of that in the kitchen but I

suppose we should get some food in you. You've been out for seven days, did you ken that?"

"Seven days? No wonder I feel weak."

"Weak for a week." Sheena chuckled at her own joke. "Come on then, let's go get you something to eat."

Chapter Four

MacLeod castle was arranged in a square. There were fifteen foot walls surrounding the courtyard with a guard tower at each of the four corners. The walls were high but they shrank into obscurity next to the huge four storey keep that dominated the space, looming above the surrounding countryside. Crows circled the roof, occasionally divebombing any pigeons that dared to emerge from their loft. Callum knew the castle like the back of his hand. He had watched his father build it when he was nothing more than a wee bairn.

He looked across to the keep. At ground level the stores were nowhere near as full as the previous year but hopefully contained enough to last the

winter. Above that the reception rooms were acces-
sible from an external stone staircase. Guests of the
castle went no further unless called up to the great
hall to see the Laird or one of his stewards. Above
the great hall was the Laird and lady's bedchamber
with further space for their servants. On the top
floor were the stairs to the tower rooms, his room,
the water tank, and the pigeon lofts.

Callum looked up at the top floor. She was
there. Why had she come? He turned away, passing
through the garden. Clothes were draped over the
bushes to dry in the last of the autumn sun. Was
that her dress? It looked like it. Was she naked up
there while it dried?

His thoughts went back to the first time he saw
her. He had marched into the keep ready to
persuade her she was better off not marrying him.
Then he saw her.

It was as if he'd never seen a woman before in
his life. He walked into the room at the top of the
east tower and there she was, asleep in the bed
they'd provided. He had been told Nessa was not
the most attractive of women, not surprising given
she was a MacKay. But what lay before him in the
bed, her eyes tightly closed, was a vision of beauty
the like of which he'd never seen. The blanket had

slumped off her body and her leg stuck out, a slender pale limb that drew his eye upward to what lay hidden behind the tartan.

He'd heard tales of fairies and sirens who lived out at sea, bewitching and beguiling men into mortal danger with their beauty. She was just like the stories. She was stunning even in repose and therein lay the risk. She wanted to trap him in marriage, force him to spend half his time dealing with MacKays. The thought was enough to make him shudder.

He had no intention of being tied down just to please his father. She might be beautiful but she was still a MacKay and an arch rival. He remembered seeing the head of his cousin on a spike outside MacKay castle. His father may have forgiven them for Lachlan's death but he did not have such a short memory.

He had an entire speech worked out but it left his head the moment he saw her. She was laid on her back and other than a small dark patch on her neck, there was no sign of injury from her fall. She did indeed look angelic in repose. Such beauty. The blanket low enough to expose a hint of her bosom.

He had talked to Sheena before going in to see her. "Found naked on the earthworks outside the tower," Sheena said. "As if she'd been dumped there or maybe fallen out of the sky. Like an angel sent by God Himself."

Callum had laughed at the idea but looking at her sleeping so soundly, he began to have second thoughts. Then she opened her eyes and he was immediately lost in them. It was only his training that stopped him kissing her in that moment. He was just about able to keep his head despite the desire that coursed through him at the sight of those sparkling blue eyes. It was a close run thing though and when he opened his mouth he was still uncertain whether it was to speak or to embrace her.

At least she agreed with him that there was to be no marriage. Perhaps she was being forced into it by her parents same as him. He left her certain the marriage would not happen but as the days passed, he could not stop thinking about her.

He marched over to the archery targets, trying to wipe her out of his mind. She'd been recovering from her head injury for a week and in that time he'd only seen her twice, once in her room and once more in the garden where she'd been helping Nessa pick herbs. The sunlight had been on her face that day and she was lit as if by a glow from heaven itself. He had stood watching her laughing and talking and he ached to go over and join in.

He swore silently. Why couldn't he get her out of his thoughts?

Rory and Ivar were lined up with their bows and he stood watching for a spell before moving over to the corner of the courtyard. In the shadow of the keep, the wooden practice swords were kept ready. Pulling one from the pile, he waved to Hamish who was leaning against the pentise, his arms folded. "Shall we get started?"

"I thought you'd got lost somewhere," Hamish replied, crossing the space to the swords and choosing one for himself. "Or were you picking out your wedding attire."

Callum jabbed at him with the sword, almost catching him before he had time to react.

At the last second Hamish swiped downward, jumping back at the same time. The blow missed him but only just. "Touchy subject I see," Hamish said, adjusting his stance.

"I'm not getting married to a MacKay so the jests can stop," Callum snapped, shifting right and swinging again.

Hamish blocked again. "Is that why you keep

looking up at her tower? To remind yourself you dinnae want her fine legs wrapping around you?"

Callum cringed. Had it been that noticeable? He hadn't deliberately been looking up there. He just glanced whenever he was passing by. If he thought about it though, he did pass by an awful lot.

The fight moved gradually into the main courtyard, the archery practice stopping while everyone turned to watch. There was a lot to learn from observing Callum in action. He moved much faster than a man his height and weight should be able to and yet at times he barely seemed to shift at all to avoid the blows. Sweat was soon pouring down Hamish's chest but it was a long time before Callum began to tire.

At last Hamish let his impatience get the better of him, lunging too far and allowing Callum to spin and catch him on the back of the leg, sending him sprawling in the mud.

A cheer went up as Callum held out a hand, helping him to his feet. "Well met," he said. "Watch that lunge next time we're out on patrol. Could get you killed."

A squire passed them both a cloth and as Callum wiped the sweat from his eyes, he looked up again at the tower. For a brief moment he could have sworn he saw a face at the window but then there was nothing.

All week it had been the same. He'd catch glimpses of her but nothing more. Why did he even care? He had enough to deal with in his father's absence. Each day began in the great hall, him on the dais, listening with the stewards to the petitions of the people, adjudicating over their disputes and trying to be fair to everyone as best he could.

He was no steward though. He was a warrior better suited to patrolling than signing contracts. He enjoyed the afternoon better, training with his men, making sure none of them were getting sloppy. One mistake out on patrol and it wouldn't be a wooden sword to the back of the leg, it would be remorseless metal biting deep into flesh.

The evening of the seventh day since her arrival was different to the routine. The horns blew out at the guard post and Callum was glad to hear them. The twin blast that echoed around the valley meant only one thing. The Laird was returning.

Let his father come back and take over the running of the place. Let him get back out on patrol where he belonged, away from the bewitching spell of Nessa up in her tower.

Dinner was not served at the usual hour. It was put back until the Laird and his lady arrived so the meal was not brought out until long after dark.

Callum sat beside his father at the top table, looking out at the mass of people enjoying their dinner. Most were in high spirits. Rumors of a wedding had begun to spread and the people were glad as it would mean an end to the bitter feud with the MacKays. Callum seemed to be the only one not enjoying himself.

"Where's Nessa?" the Laird asked, prodding Callum in the side. "There's a space there for her next to you."

"She's in her room."

"What? Eating alone? Who does that?"

"She's recovering from an injury, father."

"An injury? How the devil did that happen?"

"We think outlaws attacked her."

"Outlaws? Where? On our land?"

"She has no memory of what happened before she was found on the earthworks."

"The earthworks? So she was almost here and they attacked? I will double the patrols. Can't have outlaws reaching our walls. You've been looking after though, haven't you my boy?"

Callum nodded.

"Good. Tomorrow morning I want you both in front of me. Is that clear?"

"I willnae marry her, father. I told you."

"And I told you not to raise the subject again. You're marrying her and you better get used to the idea. Do you think I married your mother for love? Nay, I married her to double our land without a drop of blood being shed. With this one union, the MacKays become our allies and you add a patch to the MacCleod quilt."

"Love comes later," Gillian added, taking her husband's hand. "You have to work at that part."

"It's not about love," Callum replied. "I dinnae want to ever marry a MacKay. Have you forgotten about Lachlan? Your brother's son?"

"Eat your beef," the Laird said in a tone that clearly meant the conversation was over.

When the meal was done Callum found his way outside to the battlements. He stood looking out into the darkness, wondering how Moira was coping with the loss of her husband.

The shriek of her grief echoed around his head so loudly he didn't notice his mother walking up behind him until she pressed a knife to his throat

"Callum," she said, pulling the blade away. "It's

lucky I wasn't sneaking in to attack. You'd have had your throat cut by now."

"I might have welcomed it if it meant not having to marry against my will."

She put the knife back into its soft pouch at her girdle. "What is it you have against marriage? Be honest. It's more than her being a MacKay, isn't it?"

"Truthfully?

"Aye."

"I dinnae fain to leave a widow behind when I die in battle."

"You might not die in battle. Have you considered that?"

He shook his head, picturing himself shuffling around the castle in his dotage. "What? Grow old and get deaf and half blind like Jarrod?"

For a moment his mother's smile faded. "That was my father you speak of so flippantly."

He saw how hurt she looked. "I apologize mother."

She nodded. "There is no sin in growing old."

"I know but really, can you imagine it? Me an old man with a bad chest and a hunched back? There's a reason the Northmen believed only those who died in battle got into heaven. Who wants to get old and gray?"

"Old and gray like me?"

"You're different. What? Why are you smiling at me like that?"

"I'll tell you another time. Now are you coming back in? It's freezing up here."

"I'll be in shortly."

He watched her walk away before turning back to the darkness, leaning on the stone and staring out at the hidden countryside. He didn't notice it happening but soon his gaze shifted up to the east tower.

Stop thinking about her, he told himself when he realized. He headed back down to the courtyard, wondering what would happen in the morning when they were both standing before his parents. If he wasn't careful they'd end up getting him to put the ring on her finger there and then and that would be it.

He'd be wed to a MacKay and that would be the end of patrols and battles and freedom. His father would want him to secure the union with one of their mortal enemy.

Glancing up, he saw the flicker of a candle light up there. She was still awake. Why did that thought bring him joy? He shook his head, striding over to the keep and to his own chamber.

He normally fell asleep in moments but that night he lay with his eyes open for a very long time, lost in thoughts of her.

Chapter Five

I n the first week of her stay at MacCleod
castle Kerry spent her time getting to know
the place and its inhabitants. The initial
couple of days had been a whirlwind of activity.
Wherever she looked, there was noise and movement, the place crowded with people. It was
incredible.

In time she began to understand things. What
she thought was chaotic coalesced into a kind of
order. What had seemed ugly became beautiful.
What was considered beautiful in her time was
missing in many places. There were no ornamental
flowers in the garden for example. Nessa named
each of the herbs and plants growing, all of them
serving a purpose.

The kitchen was filled with functional items. Her natural interest in cooking meant she spent a lot of time in there, learning their methods and giving them some of her own. She enjoyed it most in the kitchen and the garden.

The garden was where the beauty of the place was found. The water dripping from the roof when it rained fell straight into the barrels to be used in the tanning pits. The tall undecorated walls were designed deliberately, nothing had been added that might help attacking forces or increase the cost of building.

It was so different to the castle she'd visited. Grass covered the courtyard in the modern day, paths of gravel ensuring the visitors didn't get muddy feet. There were still gaps in her memory but she recalled something happening to her in the tower.

What it was she had no clue. It was gone from her head completely. She could remember the castle, the bare walls, the fallen stones in the court-yard, the interpretation boards put up to show what building went where.

Now she could see it all as it really was. The kitchen, smoke rising from the chimney from morning to night, the fire never allowed to die out.

Next to that the chapel standing alone in the corner. There was the blacksmith's forge, the stores, the archery range, the pig pens, the tanners, the countless other stone and wooden buildings filling the space of the courtyard. So many buildings and so many people.

Everyone had a job to do. No one ever seemed to stand idle and the only rest came during dinner, itself the single meal of the day.

And what a meal it was. Lasting for hours, one course after another was brought out, each more delicious than the last, all flavored with exotic spices and dripping with sauce. They were using some of her tips but they needed little advice. The meals were magnificent.

She was even starting to learn the etiquette of the time. If you got a bone in your mouth you spat it onto the rushes behind you, not onto your plate. You only picked up food with a single finger and thumb, never the whole hand, you did not feed the dogs by hand, you tossed food to the floor for them to fight over. You wiped your mouth on the tablecloth, never your sleeve, all things she had to learn by first getting them wrong.

"Did they teach you no etiquette at MacKay castle?" Sheena asked her during her first meal in the great hall, seeing her place a bone delicately down on her trencher.

"I have forgotten much," Kerry replied, touching her head.

"Of course, I forgot about your injury. Forgive me."

She ate each night in the darkest corner of the hall, out of sight of Callum. She saw him looking for her on occasion but she remained as hidden as she could and for good reason.

From the moment he'd left her in the tower on the first day she had been unable to stop thinking about him. It was a feeling she'd never experienced before. She didn't want to see him again. She wasn't sure she'd be able to get any words out other than gibberish. Just thinking about him was enough to start her heart pounding in her chest. She wanted him like she'd never wanted anyone before. She wasn't even sure why. The only reason she could think of was that he reminded her of the Callum from her childhood dreams, a dream come vividly to life.

That was why she hid from him whenever she saw him coming. She had allowed herself a glance at him as he'd practiced sword fighting in the court-yard. Seeing him coated in sweat, his muscles bulging, she'd had to fan herself with her hand to cool down, the air suddenly stiflingly hot in the tower.

She felt like she was falling in love with him. It was ridiculous of course. They'd barely spoken two words to each other and on his side that had consisted of telling her in no uncertain terms that he wanted nothing to do with her. The fact that it was impossible to fall for someone that quickly had not stopped her doing it though.

She ached for him in a way she'd never thought possible for another human being, like she'd known him all her life even though that too was ridiculous.

She stayed away from him primarily because her feelings were too strong. Sooner or later she would find a way back to her own time and if she got too close to him, going home would become all the more painful. She was already feeling sad about the idea, leaving behind this world that no one else from her time had ever seen or would ever see again. It was just her alone that had slipped through time for a glimpse of the past as it was lived, not like in books or movies but real, and all right in front of her eyes.

Get to know him and she wouldn't be able to leave. She had to leave. This wasn't her time. What was it Doc Brown had told Marty? The slightest interference with the past could have unimaginable consequences for the present. She didn't want to get home in a year's time to find herself in a casino where the castle once stood, surrounded by biker gangs with Biff Tannen married to her mom.

Better she stayed out of the way as much as possible until she could get home. There was one thing she had to do first though and she wasn't sure how best to do it.

"You need to come downstairs."

Kerry looked across to the doorway. Sheena was standing there beckoning her.

"Why?" she replied, getting to her feet. "What is it?"

"The Laird and lady have summoned you."

"Oh." Kerry felt nervous all of a sudden. They were bound to know what Nessa looked like and would be able to tell at once that she was an imposter. The question was, what would they do then? She kicked herself for not thinking about that sooner. She'd been distracted by a juvenile crush when she should have been planning for this.

Sheena led her down the stairs to the great hall. It had been cleared of people apart from the Laird and lady. They sat together on the dais at the far end, watching as she entered the room. She winced, ready for one of them to yell, "You're not Nessa."

Neither said anything. She found her feet were not walking properly and the more she concentrated, the more certain she became that she was about to fall over, her legs feeling alien, not part of her.

Somehow she made it across the room on jelly ankles. "Sit down my dear," the lady said.

A chair was brought forward and Kerry sat, waiting nervously to see what they had to say to her.

"Where is that boy of mine?" the Laird snapped, getting to his feet and glancing past Kerry. "If I have to go fetch him-"

"I'm here."

Kerry's heart soared at the sound of Callum's warm voice. She turned her head and felt butterflies spreading inside her as he marched across the room. He didn't look at her once and she tried not to be disappointed.

It was a bit much to expect him to know how she felt. She had said nothing to him all week. She'd avoided being near him for precisely that reason. What could she say? "Hi, I'm from the future, I love you, let me have your babies." That wouldn't sound insane at all.

"My son and his bride to be," the Laird said as Callum came to sit next to her. "This is a most heart warming sight."

Kerry looked up at him. Did he really not see she was an imposter?

"I willnae marry a MacKay," Callum said. "I say you call this farce to an end and send her back to the bloodsoaked hands of her father."

"Silence!" the Laird snapped. "You will not say another word until I've said my piece and if you so much as breathe too loudly, I'll have your balls cut off and fed to the pigs."

"Alan," his wife said. "Please remember there are ladies present."

"Sorry, my dear." He turned to Kerry. "I hear you had an injury on your way here. Are you quite recovered?"

"Getting there," Kerry replied, her voice faint. Her throat felt dry as a bone left out in the desert sun. "Slowly."

"Did you get a look at those who attacked you?"

"I saw nothing, I'm afraid."

"Shame. No matter. We will catch the culprits soon enough." He turned his face to Callum. "As for you two, you will spend the next week together. You will get to know each other while we begin the wedding preparations. In seven days time you will stand before me and you will both confirm your desire to wed or you will never sleep on MacCleod land again. Do you ken?"

Callum folded his arms across his chest and stared at his father but he said nothing.

"Good. My son, I want your solemn vow that you agree to marry this lass. Is it given?"

There was a pause that lasted an ice age before Callum spoke. "Yes, father."

"Both of you can start now. Go for a walk together or something. Get to know each other."

Callum stood up and was already gone before Kerry was halfway across the room. "That boy's too stubborn for his own good," the Laird was saying behind her.

"Give him a chance," the lady called out as Kerry looked back. "His bark's worse than his bite."

Kerry managed a smile before heading outside. She found him standing in the courtyard tapping his foot impatiently. "I will not marry a MacKay," he said when she reached him. "After what your people did to my family, I can't believe he wants us to wed."

"I need to tell you something," Kerry replied. "I'm not a MacKay,"

Callum had been about to continue his rant but he stopped dead, his eyes widening. "What?"

"I'm not Nessa MacKay."

"What are you talking about? Of course you are."

"My name's Kerry Sutherland and until one week ago I'd never heard of Nessa McKay."

"What? But you were on your way to the castle. Why were you coming here if you're not her?"

"I wasn't coming here." She took a deep breath, looking him straight in the eye. "This is going to sound crazy but I'm from the future and this is going too far if they think I'm going to marry you but I'm not her. Something happened to me in my time and I woke up here. All I want to do is get home and I'm hoping you can help with that because if I stay here…" Her voice tapered away to nothing. She wanted to add, "I'll never want to leave you," but she was able to stop herself just in time. She looked up at him, awaiting the incredulous response.

To her surprise, Callum nodded. "So it's true."

"What? What's true?"

"A seer once told me I'd be visited by a lass from another time. I never believed her but here you are."

"So you believe me?"

"Aye, lass. I knew at once you were too beautiful to be a MacKay. It makes sense now. Listen, I think I know a way to solve both of our problems."

"How?"

"There is a doorway north of here."

"A doorway? What doorway?"

"Rumor came to us of a woman from the future who came through that doorway recently. And if that doorway brought her here, it must be able to take you back to your time."

"Where is it? You must take me there."

"I dinnae ken where it is but I know someone who will."

"Who?"

"You'll see. We shall head off at once. Soon you will be back in your own time and as I am betrothed to you, I cannae marry Nessa MacKay. I will have no bride to bother me any more."

Kerry kept quiet as Callum called for a pair of horses. She had no idea if he was right but what choice did she have? It was that or stay by his side and end up wanting him more than ever. Which would be fine if it wasn't for the fact his actual bride was presumably going to turn up at some point and then where would she be? Probably locked in the dungeon as an imposter and there would go her chance of a happy life with Callum.

"What about the real Nessa?" she asked.

"I dinnae know but I suspect if I sweeten the pain with news of a portal to the future, even my own father might calm down. Think what we could do with a doorway to the future. I could bring back warriors from your time and then we would have no need for a pact with the MacKays. Besides, my father made me vow to marry you. Once you're gone, the oath remains. I will be unable to marry another. Not my fault if you've vanished, is it?"

The horses were brought out and Callum climbed onto his, waiting while Kerry tried to remember the single riding lesson she'd had as a child. It took several attempts before she was up and even then she almost lost her balance twice before finally settling in place on the beast's back.

"Let's go," Callum said, turning his horse toward the gate.

Kerry tried to follow but no matter what she did her horse would not move. It just flicked its head as if she was nothing more than an errant fly irritating its ear.

"Could you give me a hand?" she shouted to Callum.

He looked back at her. "You can ride, can you?"

She shook her head in response.

"I never met a lass who could not ride," he said, bringing his own steed back to her. "No matter. We shall ride together."

With one arm he reached out and grabbed her around the waist, lifting her onto his horse, setting her down in front of him, his hand still around her waist.

"On," he called out and the horse moved forward. Kerry held her breath for a long time, feeling his strong hand holding her in place, the tips of his fingers pressing into her skin. She closed her eyes and let out her breath as slowly as she could. The quicker they made it to the portal the better.

Chapter Six

They stopped to rest after a couple of hours riding. Callum didn't want to but he could tell his companion was growing weary. Pulling the horse to a stop by a pool of clear water, he left the beast drinking its fill while laying out a blanket from the saddlebag, covering the damp earth so Kerry could sit in comfort. "I could have kept going," she said, looking up at him with her arms folded, for all the world like a petulant child.

"Aye," he replied. "And you could've fallen off and cracked your skull when your grip went."

"I was fine," she said, her voice quieter, less defiant than before. "How far do we have to go?"

"We pass between the two old men," Callum

said, pointing at a pair of jagged mountains in the distance. "There's a pass through but it's still a wee climb to the other side. After that it's only another couple of days."

"Days? I thought it'd be hours."

"What's the rush? You're in the most beautiful country in the world. I feel a part of this land and yet you wish to pass it by in a moment?"

She shrugged. "I need to get back to my own time. I can't stay here much longer."

"Why not?"

Her eyes turned away, staring into the distance. "No reason," she muttered.

He watched her closely for a moment before turning back to the saddle bag, reaching inside to bring out a lump of hard cheese. "Hungry, lass?"

"Starving."

He sliced a thick wedge and passed it over to her, taking a little for himself before leaning back against the thick trunk of an oak, watching the ripples on the pool spread as their horse stepped into the water, cooling his feet after the hard morning's ride.

Glancing across at her, he noticed once again how beautiful she looked in the daylight. The sun seemed to light up her skin, accentuating the smooth softness of her features. He could have stared at her like that for hours, drinking in her features in the same way the horse drank from the pond. Behind her the morning haze had vanished and the last of the flower was upon the heather, framing her in purple and blue.

"What?" she asked, turning to face him, a smile spreading as she saw him look away embarrassed. "Why are you watching me?"

"You seem surprised by what you see," he said, nodding in front of her. "What is it you're looking at?"

"It's this, all of this."

"What? The heather?"

"The quiet. Listen."

Callum stood still. He could hear a curlew in the distance, the water flowing into the pond, the horse splashing. Further away a stag was rutting but it wasn't in view.

"Hear that?" she asked, smiling again. "It's so quiet here. Empty too. There's no one for miles around. No planes, no cars, nothing. Just us."

"Is there no peace in your time?"

"Not according to Chamberlain." He frowned but she just laughed. "Never mind. It's just very different here."

"In what way?"

"Well, take the farms when we first left the castle."

"What about them?"

"They were divided up into strips."

"Aye. So?"

"So in my time it's just different. Never mind. Come on, we should get moving, shouldn't we?"

"I suppose so."

He didn't want to move on. He wanted to stay where he was, staring at her with the sun behind her. The spell was broken when she stood up and the perfect image gone but in its place he was able to once again enjoy her closeness. With the two of them in place on the horse, he put one hand around her waist again though he had no doubt she would not fall. She was a natural horse rider. It was in her blood. As were the Highlands.

The longer he thought about it, the more certain he became. She belonged in Scotland with him. He told himself not to think about it. What was the point of using her to ensure he did not need to marry if only to fall for her instead? He would still be wed and still unable to patrol but he would also incur the ire of his father and the wrath of the MacKays.

Behind them the castle had vanished from view. The fields and rolling heather clad glens gradually gave way to rougher country, crags and bare rocks that grew bleaker as they gained height, the track growing thin, becoming rutted. "Are we still going the right way?" she asked as the path faded away to nothing.

"Aye," he replied. "Have faith."

Another hour and they were high enough to look back and see the castle in the distance, the battlements peeking out many miles away, as if watching them go. Callum paused again to let the horse rest.

"The ravine is up ahead," he said as she looked around her. "Our land ends at the other side. We must be cautious. Bandits patrol this territory."

"Bandits?" she asked, her voice containing a hint of tension. "Will they attack us?"

"Hopefully not."

He looked ahead at the mountain pass which dwelt in the shadows. Either side the two enormous peaks acted as guardians, protecting the MacCleod land. "In ancient times, we worshipped the old men of the mountain land," he said as they edged forward slowly, the horse having to search for solid ground among the fallen stone. "Offerings were left up here for them by my ancestors. See there." He pointed at a cairn to their left. In the base a hollow had been formed and in the gloom something sparkled.

"What's that?" Kerry asked.

"A wee stone."

"A wee stone? It looks like an emerald the size of my fist?"

"Aye, maybe it is."

"And no one has stolen it?"

"It would be a rash fool who took from the old men."

"Why?"

"These mountains can help or hinder. If you want to make it through the pass alive you'd be wise to leave them an offering, not leave them angry with you."

"But-"

"Shush!" Callum held up a hand to silence her. Ahead of them a scattering of rocks tumbled down the mountainside, coming to rest in a plume of dust.

"What is it?" Kerry whispered.

"I dinnae ken," he hissed back. Glancing up at the mountainside, he saw nothing. "But I will be glad when we're through."

Urging the horse forward again, they made slow progress through the ravine, the light fading behind the mountain, leaving them in the silent gloom. There were no signs of life anywhere, only bare rocks and another tumble of stones to their right. "Is that normal?" Kerry asked.

"No," he replied. "Keep your wits about you."

He stared forward as they went, his hand going to the hilt of his sword. "Keep the reins a wee while," he whispered. "And if it comes to it, keep going forward. Ask for Fenella in the right places and many will point you the right way."

"What? Why are you telling me that?"

"Quiet. No more talk."

There was a moment of silence and then an echoing roar across the mountainside. "Bahoo!"

The response. "Bahoo!"

"What is that?" Kerry asked, twisting her neck to look at him.

"MacDonalds," he replied, spitting onto the ground as from both slopes men sprinted out from behind boulders, running as best they could down toward the two of them. "We may outrun them."

They almost made it. Snatching the reins from her, he spurred their horse onward and it stumbled through the cascading stones toward the far end of the ravine where the sunlight still shone. Would that light ever hit their skin or would they die in the shade?

As they grew closer to the end of the mountain pass, the attackers gained ground, hurling stones as they came in an attempt to make the horse throw them. "Damn them to the devil and back," Callum said. "Old men, help us."

He leapt from the horse's back and stood in the middle of the pass, sword gripped in both hands, ready for their arrival. He counted half a dozen, none of them with bows. Typical MacDonalds to mount an ambush with no bows.

"You're a dead man," one of them shouted. "And your wee lassie will be the spoils of war."

Callum said nothing response, waiting for them to get closer.

"You would spill blood in the land of the old men?" he asked when they were still a dozen yards away.

"Who believes in that nonsense?" one of them yelled back. "We've spilled many a man's blood here before and yours willnae be the last."

The stones were no longer in their favor, they had begun stumbling in their eagerness to get to him. Their lack of training prevented them working together. They were shoving each other aside, each desperate to be the one to kill the heir of the MacCleods. Kill him and they could claim Kerry for themselves. The thought was enough to clear his mind. This was what he was built for, not marriage.

He closed his eyes for a brief moment and said a silent prayer.

Then it began.

The first one to reach him tried a clumsy thrust but he batted it aside with his sword, sending the man off balance. The second made it a moment later and lifted his club, ready to bring it down on Callum's head.

By shifting his weight and leaping left, the club hit only the rock where he'd stood a moment before, smashing it in two and enraging the attacker.

Turning again, he smiled as the club ricocheted and struck the first man, sending him sprawling down to the ground.

"Let me at him," one of the others said, pushing his way through, his sword drawn. "He'll not stop me with his fancy feet." He waved the blade menacingly, marching through the others. "You're a dead man, Callum."

Callum still said nothing. Let them talk. He was patiently waiting for them to attack again.

The sword waver moved closer, the blade a blur as he shook it from side to side, his hand twisting on the hilt.

Callum managed a smile. The attacker was tiring himself out, panting heavily, his muscles bulging from the effort of constantly moving the sword.

Taking a step back, he made the attacker work harder, still not a blow had been struck. The man finally lunged at him but all his showmanship had weakened his attack and when it came, Callum was ready, flicking his own sword into the hilt of the aggressor's and sending the weapon flying into the air.

It landed several feet away and as the others laughed at his misfortune, the attacker turned and swung a punch at the nearest man. "Dinnae mock me, I do not see you doing any better."

"You couldnae do much worse."

More laughter and as the argument descended into bickering and then brawling, Callum moved slowly backward, watching them closely. Behind them on the mountainside there was a rumbling noise. Callum heard it but the others were too busy fighting each other. With another step back he had hold of the horse's head.

He swung himself up onto it, landing behind Kerry, surprised to find her crying. He had no time to ask her reasons. He needed to move. The rumbling had become a roar.

Turning the horse away, they broke into a gallop through the last of the ravine. As they went he heard the roar turn into an earsplitting crash as a boulder broke free from the very peak and rolled down into the ravine. He turned his head in time to see the boulder slam into the group of them. The noise of their bickering cut off in an instant and all he could see was dust.

"The old men do not care for blood spilled on their land," he said, turning his head and concentrating on the descent from the ravine.

"That was just a rockfall," Kerry replied. "Wasn't it?"

"What do you think, lass?" he asked.

"I don't know," she said, sniffing loudly.

"You still cry. What ails you?"

"I almost saw you get killed. We nearly died."

"Och, half a dozen MacDonalds who couldnae ambush their own mothers in a privy with a week's warning."

"Weren't you scared?"

He realized as they slowed that she was trembling, her body shaking uncontrollably.

"I will let no man hurt you," he said.

"Until I get back to my own time," she replied quietly.

He looked at the back of her neck as she continued to tremble. Someone had hurt her, he could tell. It wasn't just the fear in her eyes during the ambush, nor the tears at the danger that had befallen them. It was something deeper, something he couldn't pinpoint.

He would get them somewhere safe to rest and then he would find out just who had hurt her. Then he would track them down and make them pay for what they'd done. The thought of anyone causing her pain made him grip the reins so tightly his fingers turned white.

Behind them the old men were still. In the ravine there was no sound at all.

Chapter Seven

The slow descent from the mountain pass gave Kerry a lot of time to think. She found herself wondering if the bodies of the six men were still there in her time. Somehow her mind distanced itself from the awful human tragedy by telling her it had all happened eight hundred years ago.

Would they still be there, buried underneath that enormous boulder?

If she were to travel to that spot and dig down over the intervening centuries worth of rockfalls, would she find their skeletons still gripping rusted swords?

Her mind moved to the fall of the boulder itself. Callum had been one hundred percent certain that the spirits of the mountains had assisted him in his time of need but was it just a coincidence? There was evidence of many rockfalls up there. Perhaps the ambushers had just been unlucky. But then what a coincidence that of all the places that boulder could have landed, of all the times it could have fallen, it just happened to crush the six men trying to kill Callum?

She shook her head. It didn't matter. What mattered was that this was no fairytale Disney medieval adventure. This was real life and there were six dead bodies back there. That was bad but what was worse was knowing if they had survived, they would have done their best to murder Callum and drag her away with them. The thought of it was enough to make her shudder. Edward would have fitted in perfectly in this era. Who was Edward?

"Are you cold," Callum asked behind her.

"I'm fine," she replied. "Are you all right? Did they hurt you?"

"Not a scratch on me."

The land finally began to level out and as it did so, Callum turned the horse left, following a weak rabbit trail that headed into a wood in the distance.

"Through that and out the other side and we reach The Lantern."

"What's the lantern?"

"The inn where we will spend the night."

"And I thought you'd be a sleeping under the stars kind of guy."

"I am but you're not."

"I could sleep outside just as easily as you."

"And wake up frozen, stuck to the frost under your body?"

"Maybe an inn's not such a bad idea after all."

They rode in silence for a spell, Kerry once again becoming lost in thought. As they entered the wood, she expected to become scared of another ambush but there was no feeling of danger in there. It was strange but without all the modern buildings around she felt almost as if the landscape were talking to her.

She would never have been able to describe it to anyone from her own time but it was as if the world around her responded to things far more strongly. Callum clearly respected the land he moved through and the land respected him in return. She felt that he would never chop one of the trees down in this wood even if he were freezing to death. In return safe passage was being granted to the two of them and a sense of protection encompassed her, making her shoulders relax for the first time that day.

She didn't want to relax. If she did she might have to handle the thoughts that had whispered to her ever since the attack in the mountain pass.

Her attraction to Callum should not have grown. She had been trying to clamp down on it since they met but it was still there bubbling away and after seeing him fend off the MacDonalds in the ravine, it had wrapped around her like ivy choking a tree trunk, gripping tightly and invading her every thought.

He was a handsome man. There was no doubt about that. The confidence with which he wielded a sword stood in stark contrast to the nervousness of the attackers. The way he had moved, with no fear at all, had scared her beyond measure. She had cried not because she was scared of dying, though that fear was very real during the fight. She had cried because she feared falling into the same trap that had led to her falling for Edward.

The memory had come back all at once. Before she had woken up in the past she had been in a relationship, one that had just ended. In the time it took her to ask herself why it had ended, she knew.

He had attacked her. Not just once either. It had been a drip feed of violence that had become as much a part of her life as fetching him toast each morning, making sure it was neither burned nor underdone but just right, not easy with such a temperamental toaster as theirs was.

She felt her ribs. That pain. Was that from the fall or was that from something he had done to her? It was impossible to tell.

The tears came with the memories. She had found Edward attractive. He had been charming, witty, confident to the point of arrogance. That had all been a lie and it was one she must not fall for again.

She found one man attractive and he had become violent. It was entirely possible that she was finding this man attractive because he was violent. She knew she could not trust her own feelings, not after they had so spectacularly let her down.

The best thing she could do was get back to her own time before she fell for Callum any further. She had a proven track record of picking the wrong man and she was determined not to do it again. What she would do was get home and then put all of this behind her.

She would have a unique secret to take with her

for the rest of her life. She would have been to the past. No one else had ever done it.

No, wait. Someone else might have done it. She thought of what Callum had said, the rumors of a doorway, of someone coming from the future. What if she were to meet them? That at least would be someone she could talk to about all this.

She could not talk to Callum. If she told him about Edward, no doubt his response would be to suggest running him through with a sword.

She found herself crying again and this time there didn't seem to be any reason.

"Something ails you," Callum said. "What is it?"

"I'm fine," she replied.

"Och, you're not fine." He brought the horse to a halt and jumped down, holding out a hand to her. "We will rest here a wee while and you'll tell me what is troubling you."

She climbed down and fell into his arms, her tears turning into uncontrollable wretched sobs.

He held her against him and that just made it worse. He hadn't looked angry. He wasn't shouting at her for getting upset. He was just holding her and saying nothing at all.

"Why aren't you getting angry with me?" she

managed to ask, the words sounding ragged and interrupted by hitching breaths.

"Angry? For what?"

"For getting upset."

"Why would I get angry for that?"

She couldn't answer. She was crying again. It felt as if her tears would never stop.

When she was finally able to talk again she found herself telling him everything. Whether it was because the wood felt so safe, or because they were alone, or perhaps because she knew he could tell no one in her time about it, she shared everything. She told him about Edward, about how they met, about how he changed, how his irritation became anger and how his anger became violence.

More memories came back as she talked. He had followed her to the castle. She had been there at MacCleod castle and he had talked to her there. Had he attacked her? That was still a blank but she knew one thing for sure. When she got back home, she needed to deal with him.

Finally she was done. She sat feeling drained on a soft floor of pine needles, her legs crossed as she leaned back against a tree trunk, utterly exhausted.

Callum sat opposite her in silence. "Say something," she said at last. "Say anything. Tell me I'm an idiot for falling for him. Tell me I'm even more of an idiot for liking you. Go on, I know. I deserve to hear it."

"You're no fool," he replied quietly, his brow furrowed. "The fool was the man that saw a beauty such as a rose on a spring day and decided to stamp it into the dirt beneath. The fool was the man who ever hurt you for if I see him myself I shall have a few words to say to him and they will not be pleasant ones."

"I'm sorry, you didn't need to hear all that. You don't even know me and here I am blurting it all out. I feel like such an idiot."

"We should get moving if we are to reach the inn before nightfall."

"Yes," she said, getting to her feet. "Of course. The inn. Let's get moving."

He helped her onto the horse and she winced at his touch. She shouldn't have shared all that. He thought the worse of her and she couldn't blame him. He'd no doubt be glad to get rid of her. She couldn't exactly have made herself seem less appealing, sobbing into his chest and telling him all her woes.

Way to go, she told herself. Way to make yourself seem utterly irresistible. He'll definitely want you now.

She sat perfectly still as they rode toward the far end of the wood, following the winding path as the light began to fade. Callum said nothing. He didn't need to. Kerry knew exactly what he was thinking. He was thinking how glad he would be to finally get rid of her. She didn't blame him.

If only she could stop wanting him, everything else would be so much easier. But even with her toes curling in cringing embarrassment due to her ridiculous oversharing, she still wanted him and the thought of leaving him was still gnawing away at her.

It was not an easy ride to the inn and by the time they got there, her head was pounding. She looked at the flickering light in the distance and felt an overwhelming sense of relief. The darkness falling on the land around her had made her fear of another ambush overtake all other thoughts.

"The light," Callum said, pointing past her. "There we rest."

She did not reply. She was too busy staring at the bushes either side of them, every single one looking perfect for an outlaw to hide behind and leap out, sword drawn.

She felt as if she held her breath the rest of the way until at last the inn loomed up at them out of the darkness, a single light in an immensity of night that had swallowed the entire landscape.

"Let's go inside," Callum said, riding through an archway into a courtyard. "Find a stable boy and get something to eat."

"I'd rather have chicken," Kerry replied, pleased to see him smile in response.

He held open the door to the inn and from inside a pleasant heat drifted out. She took a final look at the dark sky before stepping inside into an entirely new world.

Chapter Eight

Callum did feel angry but his rage was not aimed at Kerry. It was aimed at the so called man, Edward, the imbecile who could take someone as delicate as her and crush her in his fist. The thought made him furious.

He knew he would never see the man. If the doorway to the future did miraculously turn out to be true, there was no way he could accompany her to her own time. He had an entire clan to look after and if he were to die there would be no heir to take over. The MacCleod name might vanish with him.

That knowledge didn't stop him wanting to go with her, track down Edward and run him through for his crimes against such a perfect woman as her.

For she was perfect. He had known that since he

had set eyes on her though he had attempted to convince himself it was not the case. He had tried to pretend he did not want her, that he could survive perfectly well once she returned to her own time.

It was not true.

It had already been too long. The chance for her to go and him to forget her, if it ever existed, was gone. He would never forget her. For the rest of his life he would retain her image in his heart, taking a place that could belong to no other even if he lived to be a hundred.

When she told him her story, he felt closer bonded to her than he ever had to anyone. He could tell she was sharing secrets she had told no one before. He felt honored.

Why had she chosen him? That he could not say. He was just glad she had at least unburdened herself of some of the mental anguish she carried.

What could he do about it though? She was going back to her own time and leaving him behind.

He thought hard.

They sat together by the fireside in the inn, waiting for the innkeeper to bring their food out to them. The fire was alive with light, the glow illuminating the smoky interior of the tavern. There were many shades of tartan on display and more accents than he could count. French, Norse, even English. No doubt every person there had a story to tell from the one eyed Saracen in the corner to the English white beard holding court with his pack of tarot cards over by the beer barrel.

Callum was only interested in one story and she was sitting opposite him and staring into the fire.

"Does the MacCleod name still live in your time?" he asked, drawing her from her reverie.

"It does," she said, turning to look at him.

He was glad. Once again he was struck by her beauty. Every time she glanced at him he was surprised, as if he had never seen her before. His desire for her grew with every passing minute. He yearned to plant a kiss on those soft lips of hers, to hold her in his arms and protect her for the rest of their lives.

He found himself hoping that perhaps the doorway was a fable, that she would have no choice but to stay with him. He could bring her back and introduce her to his parents as the only bride he would have. They would either accept that or he would ride to the ends of the earth with her and settle on a farm somewhere where no harm would come to either of them. If the Saracen could travel thousands of miles then so could they.

She smiled as he continued to look at her. "There is even a book about you."

"About me?" He couldn't hide the surprise from his voice. "Och, you're teasing me, aren't you?"

"I'm not. There's an entire series called The Saga of Callum MacCleod."

"And what does it say of me?"

Her brow wrinkled momentarily and he was again struck by the desire to kiss her. "I can't remember."

"But the name still lives. Do MacCleods still live in our castle?"

She shook her head. "That is a ruin apart from the east tower."

"The castle is a ruin?" He tried to picture it. The enormous walls that looked like they could last forever gone, the stone in moldering piles, the place empty of life. He could not do it.

"It might not be."

"What?" He looked at her closely. "What do you mean?"

"I'm not sure exactly but I think maybe I came back here to change something. I mean, what's the alternative? That a person can randomly go back through the centuries? If that were true it would be enough to drive a person insane. I get the feeling I'm here to do something and if I manage it, maybe things will be different in my time. Maybe MacCleod castle will still be standing."

"And what is it you think you have to do?"

A shadow fell over them both. Callum looked up in time to see the innkeeper carrying two wooden bowls, steam rising from the contents.

"Stew for you both and your room is almost ready for you."

"You mean our rooms?" Callum asked.

"Alas we have but one room available tonight. Tomorrow is market day at the four crosses. You picked a busy night to come and visit The Lantern."

"You do not have two rooms available?"

"You are husband and wife, aren't you? Why can you not share?"

Callum found himself trapped by his own lie.

The innkeeper walked away. "I still don't understand why you don't tell him who you are," Kerry said, looking hungrily down at her stew. You're the l-"

He cut her off. "The walls have ears and there are many here who are not so friendly as our portly innkeeper. A husband and wife draw less suspicion than any other tale I might have told. We are far from loyal land. You take the room and lock the door well. I shall sleep down here near the fire."

"No you won't. You sleep upstairs and I'll have the fireside."

He shook his head firmly. "I would not leave you alone in here for one minute. There are many already who have been looking too often in your direction."

"Then we are at an impasse."

"I suppose we are."

For a while they both ate in silence. The stew contained mostly turnips but toward the bottom Callum found a little mutton, enough to give it some flavor.

"I know," Kerry said out of nowhere. "We'll share."

"We cannot share. It would not be right."

She was already getting to her feet. "Innkeeper," she shouted. "Show us to our chamber."

Chamber was an altogether too grandiose a term for the converted hay barn they were taken to. The barn itself was attached to the inn. A set of wooden stairs led to the upper level. The stairs were worn smooth by the many feet that had made the journey before them. Upon the landing were a number of chambers running off a central corridor, the walls little more than wattle and daub in wooden frames. Callum had slept in many such places but Kerry seemed a little taken back.

He thought she was about to change her mind and demand the fireside but to his surprise she walked straight through the door held open by the innkeeper.

"It's perfect," she said, turning to face Callum as the door was closed behind them. "There's a bed big enough for two. I hope you don't snore."

"You take the bed," he said. "I will sleep here."

He pulled one of the blankets from the bed and laid it before the fire, settling upon it while Kerry continued to stand in the middle of the floor. "What are you doing?"

"Going to sleep. I suggest you do the same. We have a long ride ahead of us on the morrow."

"You're going to sleep on the floor?"

"Aye." He leapt to his feet at a sound from the landing. Glancing out, he saw only two drunken figures making their way to a room at the end of the corridor. Pulling the door closed again, he wedged the only chair against it. Only then did he return to the blanket, his sword by his side just in case.

"Oh no," Kerry said, lying back on the bed.

"What? What is it?"

"The bed's all lumpy," she replied, grabbing the blankets and coming to lie next to him. "Mind if I stay down here with you?"

He did not mind at all. He thought she might talk to him but from the moment she lay down her eyes closed. He did not sleep for some time. He sat beside her lost in thought. Looking at her made him ache with desire. The moonlight shining through the gaps in the shutters illuminated her face in gray and white. She looked like an angel.

Perhaps that was what she was. The tale of coming from the future was just that, a tale. She had been sent from heaven for some purpose he did not understand. If that were true then the feelings he had in that moment were decidedly heathen.

He lay down beside her, listening to her soft breathing, watching her chest rise and fall under the blankets. A chill breeze blew through the shutters and she shivered, turning onto her side away from him.

Without thinking about it he wrapped himself around her, holding her close. For a moment she stirred, her fingers wrapping around his. She let out a contented sigh and then fell back into a deep sleep.

Callum remained awake for sometime, breathing in the scent of her, thinking of how odd it was that just over a week had passed since her arrival. It felt as if he had known her his entire life. She had become as much a part of him as his sword arm and he would find it just as hard to cope without her as without that most vital part of his anatomy. What was a Highlander without the ability to fight? And what was he without her?

He tried to convince himself he still wanted her gone but he knew the truth. He needed her like he needed water and the mountain air. Without it he was nothing.

Eventually he closed his eyes and managed to sleep but his dreams were disturbed by a menacing figure that remained in the shadows no matter which way he looked. "I have come for her," the figure would say. "She belongs to me."

He did not know it but even as he dreamed he gripped her tighter, as if his soul wanted her to go as little as his hands. He twitched as he dreamed. At a little after three in the morning someone quietly tried the handle of the bedroom door but the chair held well and the two of them remained undisturbed. The rooms either side of them had several possessions stolen overnight but in their room, nothing was taken except Callum's heart for that had been stolen many days before.

Chapter Nine

The next morning Kerry awoke to find herself alone. She had just enough time to register where she was before the door opened and Callum walked in carrying a tall ewer. "Morning," he said, pouring water from the ewer into a bowl on the windowsill. The shutters were open and the first gray shafts of morning light were brushing the tree tops outside. "What time is it?" Kerry asked, yawning widely. "Have you been up long?"

"It is time we were moving on. Porridge is ready downstairs when we've washed."

Splashing water onto his face, Callum rubbed vigorously with his fingertips, cleaning the grime of the previous day from his features. "Are you not getting up?"

"I'm barely awake," she replied, pushing the blankets down and getting to her feet. "Just give me a second."

Dipping her hands in the water, the icy chill of it opened her eyes wide. A single splash to the face and she felt more alert than any alarm clock could have made her.

"There is talk downstairs of a thief in the inn. The Englishman from the corner last night is nowhere to be seen. I thought he looked suspicious. Come, let's get moving."

He led the way out of the bedroom and then downstairs. Kerry was glad of the thickness of her dress for the fire in the bedroom had died overnight. She wished she had a change of clothing though she seemed to be the only one to care. She noticed when they walked into the body of the inn that everyone else was still wearing what they had worn the previous night.

The patrons were all eating and talking in low voices. Someone was complaining loudly to the innkeeper that their purse of coins had been taken from their room overnight. The innkeeper was nodding patiently but saying nothing in response.

"Sit by the fire and get warm," Callum said. "You're shivering."

"Am I?" Kerry asked, looking down at her fingers, surprised to see them trembling. A few minutes by the fire and she was soon baking hot. When the porridge appeared she realized just how hungry she was, devouring it in no time at all. Callum took a second bowl and then a third and only then did he rise to his feet and go over to the innkeeper.

What they spoke of, Kerry could not make out. She found herself looking at Callum and thinking about the previous night. Was she really the same person who'd so boldly gone and laid next to him by the fireside? It wasn't even an original line she'd used, it was the one she'd seen in Twins. The fact that it had worked still shocked her. He hadn't sent her away, he had said nothing at all about her audacity. At least he was unlikely to accuse her of stealing material from a movie. The chances of him having seen it were pretty unlikely.

She couldn't believe she'd been so bold. That wasn't her. Yet it must have been. She only had to look at him to think of those arms wrapping around her, making her feel so safe as the fire died down to embers. She hadn't slept, not at first. She'd been too excited. Her heart had pounded as he held her close, his body pressing against hers. She kept as still as she could though she wanted to do so much in that moment.

She managed to control herself by telling herself she was going home soon. She would be back in her own time and she would have to learn to live without the feel of him against her, without ever smelling him again, without hearing his voice, that gruff Scottish accent of his that made her quiver with desire every single time he spoke.

Just looking at him as he talked to the innkeeper was increasing her heart rate. She pressed her hands together, trying to regain control of herself. The love she felt towards him was threatening to overwhelm her. She had to keep a handle on it if she was to get home again.

She knew one thing for certain. It would not be the same Kerry Sutherland who went home. She had already changed. Not just joining him by the fireside but everything she'd been through. She had seen death. She had seen the wildness of a land before modern invention, before pollution, before traffic, before all the things that she thought were important but they weren't, not really.

All that mattered was walking over to her and he looked angry.

"What's the matter?" she asked, immediately fearing she was the cause of his ire.

"Our horse was taken last night."

"Oh no." Kerry tried not to smile. If they had to walk it would mean longer together.

"The innkeeper is giving us another to make up for the theft. They are getting it ready now. Have you done with your porridge?"

"I have though it seems a shame to leave the fireside."

"We must be moving. The planets align soon."

"What does that matter?"

"The woman we are going to see will be away for it. We must reach her before she leaves else who knows when she may return."

Within minutes of leaving the inn it began to rain. The gray dawn never brightened. A gloom hung over them and Kerry's dress was soon soaked through. Callum continued without complaint nor pause.

The journey took most of the day. They stopped for only short spells to rest the horse and by the time the sun set Kerry was aching in places she didn't even know existed. She was barely able to walk when she finally climbed down for the last time, having to shuffle hunched over until her muscles began to relax.

They had passed through stunning countryside but Kerry had glanced at it only occasionally, for the most part keeping her head down, trying to avoid the worst of the rain.

It was an impossible task and she stood dripping wet as Callum tied up the horse to a tree trunk by the roadside. "Where are we?" she asked. "I see nothing but rain and mud."

"This way," he replied, walking between the trees and across a patch of long grass. "She lives down there."

Kerry didn't spot the cottage until they were almost on top of it. Hidden in a dip at the foot of a mountain, even the color of the walls matched the surrounding countryside, the roof made of turf with smoke rising lazily through it and drifting away into the air.

"Who lives here?" Kerry asked as they approached the cottage.

"I do," a voice said, pulling open the door to reveal an elderly woman wrapped in a tartan blanket with a headscarf hiding most of her features. "Come in, Callum," she said, beckoning them both over. "I see you've brought a wee friend with you."

"This is Kerry Sutherland," Callum said as they ducked under the doorway. "Kerry, this is Fenella. Kerry has a couple of questions for you."

"It's about the doorway, isn't it, lass?"

Kerry blinked, her eyes adjusting to the gloom as she tried to make out the interior of the cottage. "How did you know that?"

"You are not the first to come to me. Many will come. Or have come from your perspective. Time is a strange thing, dinnae you think? North corner on the left. It's like Podgorny, you think you have a handle on it and then it disappears out of the window and goes hunting mice for days. You'll have no trouble, the MacIntyres are all at their castle. Apologies, I'm rambling. You wanted to ask me something, is that right? Yes I do, it's to the north of here."

"Sorry?"

"My fault. I get ahead of myself sometimes. Ask away."

"This is going to sound strange but do you know of a door that can send people through time?"

"Yes I do, it's to the north of here."

"So we go north," Callum said.

"Go to the old hall of the MacIntyres. The door to Andrew's bedroom is the door you seek. Now Callum, go tend to my veggies. I need to speak to the lass."

Callum got up and left without another word, pulling the door closed as he went. Kerry looked across at Fenella who motioned toward a couple of battered wooden chairs. "Take a seat."

Kerry did as she was bid, feeling herself under intense scrutiny as Fenella pushed back her hood and examined her closely. "Something bad is coming for you."

Kerry sat up straight, an image of Edward flashing before her eyes. "What? What is coming?"

"That I cannot see. I only know that if you go back to your own time it will not find you."

"I am going back." She sighed with relief. "So it'll be fine."

"I have not finished. I know you are from another time and you are not the first lass from centuries hence who has stolen a Laird's heart. Know this, Kerry. You will soon have to make a choice and the choice you make will impact more people than you know."

"What choice? What are you talking about?"

"You must decide whether to stay here or return to your own time. Remain here and darkness surrounds you but also a bright light. Great things will happen to the clan as long as you make the right choice."

"And what is the right choice?"

"I do not know. Only you know that."

"But what choice do I have? I don't belong here."

"Dinnae be so sure. He's the man you love, is he not? Now you should be making a move. The planets are aligning."

She stood up and opened the door in time for Callum to walk through it. "We should be making a move. The planets are aligning," Callum said. "No doubt you want to get going, Fenella."

Kerry looked from him to Fenella. It was as if the old woman could see into the future. She had so many questions but no time to ask them. Fenella was already walking away up the mountain, leaving the two of them alone. "What did she tell you?" Callum asked as they made their way back to the roadside where their horse was waiting.

"That I have to make a choice."

"Dinnae tell me. She makes us all make choices. I dinnae know why I bother going to her. Still, at least we know the doorway is real and even better, we know where it is."

He helped her onto the horse before climbing on behind her. Slowly they continued their journey north.

"We will reach MacIntyre's old hall by morning if we dinnae encounter any of them on the way."

"Any of whom?"

"The MacIntyres. They aren't fond of MacCleods."

"Do any of the clans get on?"

"Only when fighting the English."

They did not stop once through the night. Kerry managed to doze off on a couple of occasions but the movement of the horse brought her out of sleep all too soon and by the time the sun rose she was exhausted. "It's there," Callum said, pointing past her to the stone building in the distance.

"Where is everyone? The place looks deserted."

"Remember what Fenella said? They're all at the castle which is good news for us."

Within a few minutes they were standing outside

the hall. "This way," Callum said, pulling open the door. "She said north corner on the left. I will bid you farewell here."

"You're not coming in with me?"

"The MacIntyres would start war if they found out I set foot in there." Something flashed across his eyes but Kerry could not work out what it was.

"Oh. Then I guess this is goodbye."

"Aye, lass. I thank you for your company and I wish you well in your own time." He looked like he was about to say something else but then he turned and walked away, leading the horse by the reins, not looking back.

Kerry had wanted to say so much more to him before she went but it was as if her lips had become glued shut. There was too much trying to get out and it meant nothing managed it other than a sad sigh as she turned and walked into the hall.

She could tell which doorway it was. There was the same strange energy in the air that she'd felt when she awoke on the earthworks by the castle. The door was open. All she had to do was step through and she would be back in her own time.

She thought about what Fenella had said. This was her choice to make. Stay and risk something bad but also something good. Or go back home and risk Edward. She stood looking at the door and as she did so Callum's face appeared in her mind, the way he had treated her in comparison to Edward. She took a deep breath and then made her decision.

Chapter Ten

Outside a coach roared into life, driving out of the parking lot and away from the old hall. Inside peace descended. One man was left in the building. He stood in the bedroom where Andrew MacIntyre had been born. He didn't care about the MacIntyres or Scotland. What he cared about was on the other side of the bedroom door. He looked at his watch. Any minute now.

On the other side of the door and eight hundred years before that day Kerry stood, brow furrowed as she made her decision.

The doorway waited as silent as the two people either side of it. Neither of them paid attention to the rough stones that served as both the archway between two rooms and two times. The stones hummed quietly with an energy that was barely perceptible unless you pressed your ear to them.

Taken from an ancient stone circle many centuries before, the individual pieces that made up the doorway had been hewn from a piece of solid rock in an age long forgotten. Back in those ancient days the stone circle had contained a magic all of its own. It had faded over time but a little still remained in the stones that made up the doorway into Andrew MacIntyre's bedroom.

Not all the stone from the ancient circle ended up in the old hall of course. It had spread around the Highlands. Some had made its way to MacCleod castle, used there by laborers with no idea of the power held within the rock. Two stones became part of the window frame in the east tower, the very window from which Kerry fell a week before she stood in MacIntyre hall. A week earlier and yet also hundreds of years in the future.

In the bedroom the man took a step forward, glancing down again at his watch. He had been told in no uncertain terms when she would arrive. She was late. He tutted quietly to himself. Was it possible that he had been lied to?

The two men had been convincing enough.

Kerry would walk through that doorway at exactly five past nine. All he had to do was grab her when she did, take her home where she belonged. Back by his side. Sure, he would have to punish her for what she'd done but he wouldn't be cruel, just firm. She would learn her lesson and then they would both put it behind them and get on with their lives.

He didn't give much thought to the two men who had appeared on his doorstep with the offer he'd been unable to refuse.

They had worn identical black suits and when he answered the younger of the two smiled in such a cold manner he recoiled from him.

The older one spoke. "Edward Rawcliffe?"

"I haven't seen her." He had already prepared his defense. He might have watched her fall from the tower at MacCleod castle but no one else had witnessed it. After glancing out the window and seeing no sign of her body, he'd left immediately. He was home the same day, staying there ever since. "I've already had uniform here asking about her and I'm telling you what I told them, I haven't seen her since we broke up."

"We know," the older man said, not smiling as he took a step forward. "We are not connected to the police. We work for…another party. May we come in for a moment?"

"No."

They were already inside, sitting on the sofa in the lounge as if they owned the place. The older of the two continued. "My name is Mr. Kite and this is Mr. Wint. We have an offer to make you."

"Get out of my house this minute or I call the police."

"Go ahead. I'm sure they'd be delighted to know all about you watching your ex-partner fall from a castle window to her death."

"I don't know what you're talking about."

"You needn't worry. We have no interest in informing the police in what should remain, for many reasons, an entirely private affair. Kerry did not die in the fall. Would you like to know where she is?"

"What? She's not dead?"

"Alive and well."

"So where is she?"

"Twelfth century Scotland."

Edward barked out a laugh. "Of course she is. Darning kilts and eating haggis, I bet?"

The younger man spoke for the first time. "Kilts were not invented until the sixteenth century."

The older man waved him into silence. "Now is not the time to give the man a history lesson."

Edward tapped his foot impatiently. "Come on, this is a joke, isn't it?"

"I assure you we are deadly serious, Mr. Rawcliffe. We would like to make you a most generous offer and we ask only one thing in return."

"What? What kind of offer?"

They didn't tell him straight away of course. Instead they went on for ages about determinism and causality and fixed times in space and all kinds of things he didn't understand. He nodded along until they finally got to the point.

If he went back to Scotland and stood inside Andrew MacIntyre's bedroom in MacIntyre Hall at five past nine the next morning he would see Kerry walk through the door. All he had to do then was take her home and keep her there. A happy ending for him and Kerry and he would never see Mr. Kite or Mr. Wint ever again.

He agreed of course. Something about the way they spoke over the course of the hour they were in the house convinced him they were telling the truth. It was only when he stood in MacIntyre Hall the next morning and his watch told him it was six minutes past nine that he began to wonder. Had he been duped?

According to them she had fallen out of the tower and slipped back in time to the twelfth century. It had seemed so convincing but the more he thought about it the more stupid it sounded. It was nonsense. She wasn't coming through time back to the present.

She was dead and this was some kind of set up to try and get him to confess to killing her. It wouldn't work. He hadn't killed her. She had fallen out of the window because she was as clumsy as she'd always been. That was hardly his fault, was it?

"Screw this," he said when his watch reached eight minutes past nine. He walked out the door into the corridor. He'd been conned. Very funny. He would get home and have some choice words to say to them two if they turned up at his house again.

He stopped dead when he saw someone in the distance. A woman was walking out the front door into the morning light. It was her, he was sure of it.

She wasn't in the past but she was in the hall. What was more, she hadn't spotted him yet.

He crept toward her as she headed outside.

Reaching the doorway a few seconds after her, he watched as she crossed the grass.

Wait. Grass? Why was there grass outside? Had he got lost in there and come out by a different entrance?

It didn't matter. What mattered was that the woman he loved was running after a man in bizarre clothes, a man who was turning to face her with a smile on his face. Beside the man, a horse stood patient.

Edward wanted to kill the horse and the man. How dare he smile at her? Jealousy flared inside him.

"I'm staying," Kerry said, her voice loud enough for him to hear from the doorway. "I want to stay, Callum. With you. If you'll have me. I...I love you."

The jealousy inside Edward began to boil over, turning into white hot rage. She loved that...that mud splattered bum over there?

"I love you too," the man said, taking hold of her hands. How dare he touch her?

Edward didn't hear anyone coming up behind him until he felt a tap on his shoulder. "A word," a voice said in his ear. "Before you do anything rash."

"Rash?" he said, spinning around to find

himself facing the two men who'd sent him to Scotland in the first place. "You told me she would run back into my arms. Look at her."

"You were supposed to wait in the bedroom for her," Mr. Kite said. "It is not our fault if you cannot follow simple instructions."

"Hey," Edward snapped. "I did as you said. She didn't come through. How is that my fault?"

"What?" Mr. Wint sounded shocked. "Are you sure?"

"I gave it until ten past and nothing. It was only when I left that I saw her.

The man turned pale, muttering to his colleague. "How was that possible?"

"She is far from her path," Mr. Kite replied before realizing Edward was staring at him. "No matter. He can still get her."

"No I can't," Edward said, looking outside again. "They just rode off on his horse together like it's the end of a western."

"Then you better be after her, hadn't you?"

Edward shook his head. "I'm not going anywhere until you explain to me why this matters so much to you two."

"It matters not one whit to either of us."

"Then why are you shoving me after her? What's in it for you?"

"You might as well tell him," Mr. Kite said.

Mr. Wint sighed. "You saw the man she rode off with, correct?"

"The bum?"

"That bum was heir to the entire MacCleod clan and he just rode off with your partner to live happily ever after in his castle. Are you not concerned?"

"His castle? What is this, Game of Thrones?"

"No. This is twelfth century Scotland and you are wasting time. Go after them and get her back."

"Not until you answer my question. Why do you care so much?"

The two men looked at each other before turning to face him again. Mr. Wint spoke. "Very well. Callum MacCleod is betrothed to Nessa MacKay. Our employer wishes for the wedding to go ahead and the odds of that are somewhat diminished if your partner remains with Callum. Do you understand?"

"Oh, I get it. Your boss is Nessa's dad, right?"

"That's not important right now. You need to find a horse and get after them."

"And what do I do when I catch them?"

Bring Kerry back with you to the twenty-first century where she belongs. Leave Callum to marry Nessa as planned and everything goes back to the way it should be."

Edward smiled to himself. He would bring Kerry back all right. That would be simple enough. She was weak willed and easy to persuade. That was what had drawn him to her in the first place. He had always been attracted to the gullible, those he could manipulate into becoming reliant on him. The fact that she had been the first one to leave him only made her all the more desirable. She wouldn't leave him again.

"Are you coming?" he asked, stepping out onto the grass. They didn't move. "You can't, can you? You can't leave the building. Why not?"

The two men glared at him. "We cannot interfere with the past directly," Mr. Wint said. "Just be sure you get her back to your time within the next forty-eight hours. They will stay at a tavern called The Red Wolf tonight. It is twenty miles south of here. You should get moving if you want to get her back. Remember, leave Callum alone. He must marry Nessa as planned."

"I'll get Kerry back," Edward replied, not adding that he had no intention of leaving Callum to marry another woman. The man had set hands on his woman.

He set off walking, not looking back. He would catch up with them soon enough. After all, he had true love on his side. That and the wickedly sharp flick knife he kept in his back pocket. With both he had no doubt at all that he would succeed. Present, past, future. Who cared really? What mattered was that she learned her lesson and that Scotch prick learned to keep his hands off another man's woman.

Behind him the two men walked back to the bedroom. "Will this work?" Mr. Wint asked as they went. "Time is against us."

"Isn't it always?" Mr. Kite replied, walking through the doorway and vanishing as if he'd never been there. But of course he was there. He had just taken one step through space and eight hundred years through time. His companion followed a moment later.

Eight centuries earlier, Edward headed south.

Chapter Eleven

Callum could hardly believe it. One minute he was trying to get his head around the concept of never seeing her again, the next she was by his side, telling him she loved him.

She sat in front of him on the horse, blanket around her shoulders to keep out the chill wind as they headed south. Callum kept one arm around her, the other holding the reins of the horse.

She leaned back against him and sighed. He felt the softness of her hair on his cheek as he held her closer. It was hard to believe it was true but she had said it. She loved him.

It had been so different when they'd arrived at

the old hall. He had told her he couldn't step inside because of the MacIntyres but the truth was he just couldn't do it. He couldn't bear to watch her vanish in front of his eyes.

She hadn't vanished though. She was still there, leaning back against him.

"What are you thinking?" she asked, glancing up at him.

"What to tell my parents. I'm presuming the real Nessa has turned up by now."

"Oh yes. I'd forgotten about that."

Callum had too. It was only when they were riding that he remembered he was supposed to marry Nessa MacKay.

"What do you think they'll say?" Kerry continued. "When you tell them, I mean."

"They'll tell me that I can't marry for love."

"Oh." Kerry lapsed into silence.

Callum thought hard about the best way to handle things. He had absolutely no intention of going through with the wedding to Nessa, not with Kerry making the supreme sacrifice of forgoing her own time to be with him. "Will you miss the future?" he asked, breaking the silence that had fallen between them.

"Not really. I'll miss my mom I guess but I know she'd understand if I told you where I was. I would miss you much more. Besides I like it here."

Silence fell again. Callum didn't mind the quiet. All that mattered was the woman he loved was by his side.

Doubt only began to enter his mind when they approached The Red Wolf late that evening. He thought about what he'd told his men. A Highland warrior who married should no longer patrol. A Highland warrior who patrolled should not think to marry.

He had told his father he would not marry Nessa because he did not want to leave a grieving bride behind if he was killed in battle. Why would the same rules not apply to Kerry?

He wanted to marry her though. He wanted to be by her side for the rest of his life. From the minute he'd met her, he'd seen something different in her, something he had never seen in another woman. Perhaps it because she was from the future. More likely it was something unique about her.

Marrying her was not going to be easy. Go through with it and a rift would open up between the MacCleods and the MacKays, one that would probably end in clan war. His father might disown him too. He might never become Laird.

He shook the doubts away. They didn't matter. All that mattered was right there, climbing down from the horse in the courtyard of the inn. She smiled up at him and he melted inside. "Why are you looking at me like that?" she asked, still smiling.

"Because you look more beautiful in the moonlight than any lass has a right to look."

She laughed as a stable boy ran over. "Look after this one," Callum said to the boy, pressing a coin into his hand at the same time. "Belongs to the landlord of The Lantern. He'll want it well treated."

"Of course, my Laird," the boy said, the coin already gone.

Callum led the way through the door of The Red Wolf. Inside they hit a wall of heat coming from the enormous fireplace. The place was busy. There were only a couple of empty tables. No one seemed to notice them enter though and they were soon squeezed in the far corner near the shuttered window.

"Callum MacCleod," a voice said as they sat down. "It's been a long time."

Callum looked around in time to see an enormous grizzled man with a shock of red hair that stood strained on end like it was trying to fight its way off his head. The man approached them slowly, squeezing between the tables, his gut brushing the wood as he maneuvered his way over. "Angus," Callum said. "I havenae seen you since the last clan council. How's Belle?"

"Gone off to Loch Leven land to learn letters."

"Lovely," Kerry said. "I bet she'll have an 'L' of a time."

Angus gave her a glance before turning his attention back to Callum. "What are you doing on MacIntyre land? I hope you're not looking for trouble. I've enough to deal with without any brawling."

Callum shook his head. "All we want is food and a room for the night. We'll be gone at first light."

"I can do you some stew but the joint's all been had. We've had a busy day."

"Stew will do fine. Coney?"

"Aye."

"And the room?"

"Up and end of the hall on the left. Fire's already lit."

"We are in your debt."

Coins were exchanged and then Angus left them, returning almost at once with two steaming wooden bowls. The smell of food made Callum's stomach rumble. He hadn't realized how hungry he was until the stew was in front of him.

After they'd eaten, they made their way to the bed chamber. Inside was dark, lit only by the glowing fire. Callum found a candle and pushed it toward the flame, catching the wick enough to cast a little extra light to the bedside. "One bed," Kerry said, running her hand along the blanket. "Whatever will we do?"

"I shall sleep on the floor," Callum replied. "You take the bed."

"You don't want to sleep with me?" In the time it took her to ask she had moved across the room and slipped her hands into his. "My Laird?"

He couldn't resist kissing her. The softness of her hands, the way she looked in the glow of the fireplace, the scent of her body in the small bedchamber, it was all too much. It was a sin but he could not resist.

He wrapped his arms around her, pressing his lips to hers. It was a perfect kiss, his body responding at once.

Shaking his head, he forced himself away from her.

"Why…why did you stop?" she asked, looking hurt. "Did I do something wrong?"

"Nay, lass," he replied. "But it is not proper. We must do no more until we are wed."

"What? Oh, of course. I understand." She was no longer looking at him.

"Do you? You sound angry."

"I'm not angry. I'm just tired. It's been a long day and I'm not used to all this horse riding. Let's get some sleep."

"I shall fetch some water to bathe." He turned and left the room.

He walked back downstairs and found an empty table in the corner. Sitting down, he leaned back, staring at the room full of people but seeing none of them. Did she know the water was only an excuse? That he needed to think?

Why had she looked like that? Why had she sounded so angry? It didn't make any sense. Did she not want to do things the proper way?

"I know why you're looking like that."

He looked up to find himself looking up at a man in strange clothes smiling warmly back at him. "This is because of Kerry, isn't it?" the man continued. "Mind if I take a seat?"

"Who are you?" Callum asked as the man

dragged over a chair and sat down opposite him. "How do you know Kerry?"

"I should know her. I'm her husband."

"What?"

"I know, I know. She's lied to you like she's lied to lots of men. You weren't the first to be fooled by her and you probably won't be the last."

"You're her husband? Where's your ring?"

"She took it with her when she ran off. Fourth time she's done that. Costs me a fortune to keep getting them remade. She's ill, you see. In the head. She does this stupid thing, been doing it ever since she was little. Wanders around telling everyone she's from the future. Complete nonsense of course. Has she asked you for any money yet?"

"No, why?"

"Good, that means I found her in time. The amount she's taken from people like you over the years. Don't get me wrong. I don't hold anything against you. She can be very convincing. What did she say to you? Let me guess. She loves you not because you're heir to a clan fortune but just conveniently for you? Almost left you then didn't go back to the future and instead stayed with you for true love?"

Callum found himself nodding. "Aye. She did say that."

"There is no portal to the future. It's just part of her...her malady. You can leave her with me now. I'll make sure she gets the help she needs. I've prepared a horse for you. It's better that way. Some people can get...angry when they find out they've been duped by her and we wouldn't want to hurt her, would we? Not when she's ill. She doesn't mean it, you see. Just imagine how I feel? I have to keep chasing her and bringing her home when she goes off after all these different men. I'm not the jealous type though. I'm just glad I got here before it was too late. What is the punishment for bigamy these days?"

"You're telling me to leave her here?"

"I'm not telling you to do anything. You're welcome to stay but whenever she sees me, she knows her fun is over. She can say some hurtful things, you see. Liable to hurt you when all you did was fall for her lies. I'm going to go get her and take her home. Do you want to stay to see her swearing and spitting everywhere? I bet she told you I'm the violent one, right?"

Callum nodded, realizing. "You're Edward, aren't you?"

"Let me guess. I'm her violent ex partner from the future?"

"Aye."

"Realize how strange that sounds? That me and her are from the future? She projects her violent tendencies onto me, makes it out as if I'm this awful person because she becomes an animal when she's caught with a new victim. Best you go and leave me to deal with her. I've done it plenty of time before. You get yourself home and no one need know what you fell for."

Callum was no more than a few hundred yards down the road when he stopped. Something about this didn't make sense. Fenella had told them about a portal to the future. But then she had talked to Kerry alone for a long time. Was it about this? Was this the truth? He hadn't seen the portal. Kerry said she almost went through it but maybe the reason she hadn't was because it didn't exist.

She had told him nothing solid about the future. It was entirely possible she had made it all up. But why? For his money? No, that didn't feel right.

The man had been utterly convincing but something wasn't right.

He wanted answers and he kicked himself for leaving. She was probably still there, fighting off her husband and refusing to leave. He had chance to put some questions to her before they went. Find out the truth.

What was more likely? That the woman he had known for the last week was telling the truth or the strange man he'd just met? There was only one way to find out if he'd just been tricked or not. He would go back and speak to her for himself.

She wasn't there. The bed chamber was empty apart from a note that had been left in the middle of the bed.

I cannot see you any more. I am sorry for hurting you. Do not come after me. Kerry.

He read it four times before cramming it into a fold of his baldric. She had gone. She didn't want to see him anymore.

He sank onto the bed and tried to process everything that had happened in the last hour. He'd gone from blissfully happy and thinking he was going to marry the woman he loved to completely alone.

Eventually he got to his feet, making his way slowly to the door. Once he was outside he climbed onto his horse, feeling numb. He rode slowly south.

It was time to go home and get married like his

parents had planned. Falling in love had only brought him shock and pain. Better to marry for the sake of a clan alliance like they wanted. Love could remain the domain of the bards who could sing of it while never knowing the damage it caused. He wanted nothing more to do with it.

Chapter Twelve

✦

Kerry felt utterly miserable. The walk north in the dark was freezing cold but that wasn't why sorrow seeped into her bones.

Callum didn't want her.

It was so obvious when she thought about it. She had tried to kiss him and he couldn't leave the room fast enough. He'd obviously been able to keep the act going while he thought she was going home, not wanting to hurt her feelings by telling her he didn't want her. Then she made the stupid mistake of staying and telling him she loved him.

How had he reacted? Told her the same and then presumably sat in a blind panic on the horse trying to work out how to get rid of her.

Edward had come along at the right time. She was clearly supposed to be with him, not with Callum. This was her destiny. Traveling hundreds of years back in time and Edward had still found her. As he'd said, they were meant to be together.

He hadn't even yelled. Not once. He'd been sympathetic instead, hugging her and telling her it would be all right.

One kiss with Callum and he scarpered out of the door and straight out of the tavern. She only found out the truth when Edward knocked on the bedroom door.

She almost screamed when she opened it, seeing him standing there. "What have you done with Callum?" she managed to ask, already wincing, expecting a fight.

"Nothing at all," Edward replied, passing her a note. "He asked me to give you this though."

She unfolded the piece of paper and read it. It didn't take long, consisting only of two words.

Go home.

"What does it mean?" she asked, unable to take in the words.

"He didn't deserve you," Edward said, stepping

forward and taking the note from her. "Do you want to know what he said to me?"

She nodded although she didn't really want to know. She was too numb to take in much of anything.

"I saw him in the bar, laughing with the others down there. Said he'd only wanted to get you into bed but couldn't go through with it when he realized how fat and ugly you are. Can you believe he'd say that?"

"He said that?" Kerry asked, her voice little more than a whisper. There was a hint of hope to it, as if she wanted to believe it wasn't true.

"I love you for who you are," Edward said, slipping his hands into hers. "You know that, don't you?"

Kerry was still numb. She was barely aware of his guiding hands as he took her downstairs and out the back door of the tavern.

As they walked north together in the dark, Edward continued holding her hand, saying nothing until the lights of the tavern had vanished far behind them. Only then did he speak. "I left him a note," he said. "Told him he didn't deserve someone as beautiful as you." He squeezed her hand. "And you are beautiful, Kerry. Or at least you will be once you get out of those filthy clothes and into something more sensible."

"Where are you taking me?" Kerry asked, looking up at him as he smiled in the gleam of the moonlight. "Where are we going?"

"We're going home," he replied. "Back where we both belong. Put the past behind us. Literally."

"But what about Callum?"

"You mean am I angry about you running off with another man?" He shook his head. "I know I have every right to be angry but I'm not. I understand exactly why you did it, Kerry."

"You do?"

"Of course I do. You thought you were stuck here in the past so you tried to make the best of it. Latched onto the first person who complimented you, isn't that right?"

"No, that's not what happened. I-"

He cut her off. "Yes it is but that's okay. I don't mind. Once we get home, we can just forget about it and carry on as before."

"But…" Her voice trailed away to nothing and the sorrow began to seep into her. He was holding her hand too tightly for her to break free. Was it even worth trying? Where would she go? Into the mountains to starve to death? Callum didn't want her. He had told her to go home.

She thought about their kiss. It had felt perfect. The feel of his lips on hers, the warmth that spread through her, the sensation that she had always been half of something and when they kissed, that half had connected with the missing half and she was made whole. She never wanted that feeling to go but within moments it was wrenched from her.

She had been so certain that she understood him. For the first time in her life everything seemed right. Then he pulled away, making up some nonsense about waiting until they were married.

That might have been true, she supposed. If only he hadn't then run out of the room like a scalded cat.

Her shoulders sagged as she walked. What was the point in trying to fight her fate?

What was it that Fenella had said? If she chose to stay in the past darkness would come? Was that it?

Darkness had come. It had washed over her like a wave and now it was suffocating her like a thick blanket over her face. She could hardly breathe through it. Tears would not come, the sensation was too much. A numbness was spreading through her, a numbness she remembered all too well. It had been there whenever Edward had hurt her in the past, a way of switching off, trying to ignore the pain he'd caused.

She listened as he continued talking, his words worming their way into the most vulnerable parts of her mind, taking over, making her see that he was right. He had punished her because she had been bad but he was magnanimous. He would forgive her for what she had done while she was here. He was compassionate. He would let it all go.

The one thing he would not let go was her hand. He continued to keep tight hold of it the entire time they walked north.

As the hours passed she began to tire. She'd become used to traveling by horse and so many miles on foot in the icy chill was exhausting.

Stumbling yet again, she almost fell. Edward turned to look at her. "You need to rest," he said, smiling patiently. "Sit here for a minute."

She was barely on the ground before she was asleep. When she next opened her eyes the sun had risen and Edward was stretching his arms next to her, yawning loudly. "Where did this blanket come from?" she asked, gripping the heavy wool that was draped over her body, keeping out the worst of the cold.

"Bought it from a cottage while you slept," he replied. "I know, you're grateful. Don't mention it. I intend to do things differently when we get back, not take you for granted like I did before you went. Things will be all right between us this time. We just need to get back to our time with beds and central heating and none of this walking everywhere. I swear we could have driven from the inn to the old hall in about half an hour if we had a car."

"Is that where we're going?" Kerry asked, getting slowly to her feet, keeping the blanket wrapped around her.

"Unless you know of another way back to the future?"

"No but how do you know about it?"

"I followed my heart and it brought me to my true love. That's you, Kerry. You know I love you, don't you?"

She nodded slowly, unable to meet his eyes. She was afraid of what she might see in them.

The morning sun took away the worst of the cold but it was still a chill day as they began once again to walk north. In the daylight Kerry could see where they were. She recognized the mountains to her left from the last time she came this way. By her calculations they only had a couple of hours to go before they'd reach the hall.

What then?

She would walk through and go back to her old life. She would go back and be with Edward.

She didn't want to do it but she had established that she wasn't going to get to do what she wanted. What she wanted was to be with the man she loved but it turned out he didn't want her.

She didn't ask herself if it was possible that Edward was lying. Even if he was, he had nothing to do with the fact that Callum had left the room immediately after they kissed and he had not come back.

Nor had he been downstairs in the tavern when she left. He had left her at once. No doubt he was on his way back home to marry the woman he was supposed to.

Was that why he'd done it? She allowed herself a spark of hope. Perhaps he had felt something for her but he was as much a victim of circumstance as her. He had to marry Nessa for the sake of his clan. She was a splinter, something irritating to be removed before it could do too much harm.

Was that true though? The question she hadn't

asked herself came loud and clear to her. What if Edward was lying?

She looked at his face and at once the warmth left it. That was just a mask. He was smiling still but his hand was once again holding hers tightly.

She shook her head. How had she fallen for it yet again? She could have kicked herself. The only explanation was how tired and cold she'd been last night, too chilled to the bone to think clearly. She'd also been thrown by Callum running out on her, dwelling on that when she should have been thinking.

"Not long to go," Edward said, glancing at her. "Then we'll get home and everything can go back the way it was."

Of course, she thought. Back how it was. Her under his thumb, obeying all his rules, never being allowed to have a mind of her own. Callum had never once struck her, had never once shown an iota of violent motion toward her. Callum had been far kinder to her than Edward ever had. That didn't explain why he left after the kiss but maybe he really had just gone to get some water. That would explain why he hadn't been in the tavern when she descended the stairs.

What about the note though?

"What have you done with him?" she asked, realization hitting her in a wave.

"With who?" Edward asked, his voice light and unconcerned. She knew that voice. He was hiding something,

"I know you wrote that note. What have you done with Callum?"

"All right, you got me. I wrote the note but it was for your own good."

"Where's Callum?"

He looked angry for the first time since he'd found her in the tavern. "Oh, Callum, Callum, Callum. Why are you so obsessed with a man who ran off like a coward as soon as I turned up?"

"It's not true, is it? He didn't say I was fat or ugly, did he?"

"Does it matter? He's gone and I'm here and I'm taking you home."

"I'm not going home with you, Edward." She tried to pull her hand free from his grip but he wouldn't let go.

"Yes, you are." He smiled as he saw her looking around her. "Go ahead and scream for help. There's no one around for miles. You scream then I break a couple of your ribs for your trouble and then you still come home with me. Wouldn't it be

146

better all right if you stopped fighting and accept it? We are meant to be together."

"No we're not."

He leaned close to her face, any hint of a smile gone. His eyes were cold, his voice a whisper. "Walk or I kill you, Kerry. I've had enough of your bull. Trying to run off with another man like I'd let you get away with it? You're stupider than you look." His voice returned to normal as he yanked her by the arm, pulling her along the road. "Don't worry though. I forgive you."

Chapter Thirteen

MacLeod castle was usually a welcome sight. Many times when Callum returned from patrols he had been glad to see its towers and flags soaring, the crows circling, the white walls that spoke of power and strength to any that might threaten the clan. He had always felt that he was coming back to a safe place when he returned.

Not this time. His home felt neither safe nor welcoming. For one thing he was coming back without Kerry. For another, he knew he was going to have to deal with the aftermath of his ill fated journey north to MacIntyre hall.

Was it possible they had heard of him straying onto the land of another clan for no good reason?

Could he even explain it if he were asked? I went onto their land to assist a woman from the future with getting back to her own time.

What about Nessa? Would she be there waiting for him?

He sat on the back of his horse and looked down the slope at the castle. There it was, looking much like it had done the last time he saw it. The castle had not changed but he definitely had. So much had changed since he went north with Kerry.

It had been two days since he left The Red Fox and in that time he had tried not to think of her, to think only of returning home and putting all that behind him.

He was a warrior, that was all. A Highland warrior who never doubted himself. What would his men think if they'd seen him looking so glum on the trail south? They would have thought he'd been bewitched and in many ways he had. Not any more. That time was gone.

He allowed himself a last few moments of peace. When he entered the castle there would be little peace for a long time, if ever again.

The flags flying high gave away signals to those who knew how to read them. His parents were home, that was the most important thing to know. It meant there was no avoiding the inevitable. It was going to be marry Nessa or be banished.

He had no intention of being banished. That would be like having an arm wrenched off, a part of him torn from his body that might leave him alive but he would not be living.

There was no choice but to marry her. Kerry did not want him. That had been made abundantly clear with the note she'd left for him. He had been a fool to open himself up to her. He would have been better never meeting her, remaining on patrol forever, protecting the clan with his sword rather than risking its safety over a woman.

He had been wrong to fall for her and it wasn't something he would do again.

He sat taller on his horse. He would marry Nessa as they deigned but he would not remain by her side. With no love between them she would not mourn him if he died in battle.

Dying in battle was exactly what he had planned. As he began to ride down the slope to the castle, he couldn't think of a better way of ending the pain of losing Kerry than by a sword running him through as it had done to Orm.

The pain of conflict was nothing to the pain he felt deep inside and as he rode closer to his home he did his best to leave all thoughts about Kerry on the mountain behind him. He was not meant to love. He was meant to be Laird. He was meant to protect his people. That was his destiny. Getting involved with a woman who pretended she was the future was foolish but at least nobody here knew about it.

There must have been someone watching out for him because by the time he reached the castle gates his father was standing there, arms folded. "Who was she?" he asked as Callum nodded a greeting.

"Who?"

"You know who, my lad. The woman you ran off with. Who was she?"

"Nessa MacKay."

"So who's that over there then?" He pointed into the courtyard. Callum walked past him, knowing what he would see. At the far side of the courtyard an elderly man was standing deep in conversation with a young woman. Both of them were wearing the tartan that Callum knew all too well.

Callum winced. "That's Nessa and old man MacKay."

"Nessa and her father, aye laddie, that is them.

Perhaps you might tell me again who you went north with."

"Just a lass I met."

His father's eyes narrowed before he burst out laughing. "Good God, dinnae let your mother find out."

"Find out what?"

Alan threw an arm around his son, lowering his voice. "I ken what it's like. You want to get to know the lassies for a wee while before you settle. Dinnae forget I was young once. I dinnae judge you for it but now's the time to become a man, not a laddie. Come on in and meet your bride to be and we'll say no more about any of this."

Before they could cross the courtyard Nessa and her father vanished inside the keep, Nessa glancing back over her shoulder and giving Callum a look of undisguised contempt.

"Should we follow them?" Callum asked. "She does not seem that pleased to see me."

"Only because you are encrusted with filth and she has been waiting these six days for your return. Let her have her time in anger. You get yourself clean and then you will meet her tonight at dinner. We will have a feast to celebrate your return."

"Can we afford a feast, father? Are we not still planning for winter shortage?"

"You have a lot to learn about politics, my boy. We must show them our stores are bulging."

"But they aren't."

"No but when MacKay goes home, he can tell his clan we are struggling and might be easy to conquer. Or he can go back and say he ate a feast fit for kings and they should accept we are the better clan."

"Why can we not just share out the food with those who are hungry? I passed many struggling villages on the way home, father. They would be glad of what we have to spare."

"Did you not hear me? It is not spare. It is to impress MacKay. Now go to the infirmary and wait."

Callum crossed the courtyard on a path of rushes, the mud crunching underneath as the last of the morning frost melted away in the weak sunlight. Inside the infirmary was dark, the smell pungent, mint and lavender perfuming the air. The beds were empty which was fortunate.

The Laird might be happy bathing with the sound of the dying around him but Callum could never enjoy cleaning his body with the sick just feet away. He wanted to tend to them, not indulge himself. He could never distance himself from his people in the same way his father could.

They were different in many ways. He would never dream of marrying a MacKay if it were up to him. Not after what they did to Lachlan.

What was it his father told him? He had a lot to learn about politics.

The bath was sunken into the floor in the infirmary warming room. Tiled and beside the enormous fireplace, it was modeled on the bath found in the model of a Norman bishop his grandfather had visited once many decades earlier.

It was four feet deep, the tiles glazed and colored to match the MacCleod tartan. The jugs were sitting by the fire warming slowly. He picked up the first one, ignoring the heat that scorched his fingers. Pouring it into the bath, he watched it pool at the bottom, steam rising slowly.

"We will do that for you," a voice said behind him. That was another difference between him and his father. He didn't want servants doing everything for him. He wanted to fill his own bath.

Nonetheless, he let them do it. He was tired of arguing. He was tired of everything. He sat sweating by the fireside as the servants filed out carrying the empty jugs with them.

Stripping out of his clothes, he sank into the hot water and ducked underneath it, letting it soak into his pores. Coming up for air a few moments later, he pushed his hair back from his forehead, leaning back against the tiles, rubbing the dirt from his skin.

He refused to think about Kerry anymore but she invaded his feelings anyway, a more insistent warrior than any he had ever fought, overcoming his defenses effortlessly and whispering to him in a voice he could not hear.

What was she saying to him? He did not know but he cursed under his breath, telling himself to put her from his mind.

He needed to think about the future and she wasn't it. Nessa was his future. She might have looked as if she wanted to kill him when she first saw him but that wasn't so bad. It would make it easier when he told her he had no intention of ever sleeping with her.

The water remained heated by the enormous fireplace. He needed only to climb out when he was done and that wouldn't be any time soon. In here, he was alone, or so he thought.

"Callum," a voice called out.

"Bathing," he shouted back. "Leave me be."

Fenella appeared a moment later. "I heard you were back."

"Aye but you apparently didnae hear me say leave me be."

"Good to see you too. I come all the way here to see you and that's how you greet me. You might want to cover that by the way."

Callum glanced down at the water, placing his hands over his lap as he realized. "Why are you here, Fenella?"

"I came to ask where your woman might be found."

"In the keep."

"Not Nessa. Your woman." Fenella held her hands to the fire to warm them. "It is bitter out there," she added.

"She lied to me, Fenella."

"What about?"

"I dinnae have any wish to talk about it no more."

"So you're going to marry Nessa then and that's that?"

"I suppose so. What? Why are you looking at me like that?"

"Because you're a fool, Callum MacCleod." She

knelt next to the tub and looked at him closely. "You have a question to ask me. Come on, out with it."

Callum ran a hand through his hair before speaking. "What did you talk to Kerry about while I was out tending your veggies?"

"I know what answer you seek, Callum but only you can find it. You cannot be led by the hand all your life. You have to make the choices that matter if you are to be the Highlander I know you can be." She pressed a hand to his shoulder. "Do you want a life with a stranger who might be lying to you or a woman who hates you?"

"That's no choice. Kerry's gone."

"Has she?"

"Do you know something I dinnae?"

"I only know she has choices to make same as you."

"But she lied to me, didn't she?"

"Lies and truth are not as far apart as some might wish. I could tell you I came here today to bless your wedding. To you that is a lie, to your parents it will be the truth. Do you see they can be different but the same depending on who is listening?"

"No. I dinnae see at all. Why can you not give me a straight answer to my questions?"

"For the same reason I dinnae raise an army whenever danger beckons near my wee cottage. I am not taking charge of your life nor any life. I am just an old woman who likes her peace and I only came to bid greeting to a man in a bath."

"And I'm a man who is done with his bath so if you'll excuse me."

She nodded, getting to her feet. "I shall see you at dinner this evening."

She was gone without a sound leaving Callum to climb out of the bath and dry himself by the fire. He looked down at his body, examining the damaged skin, the bruises, the scars from a lifetime of conflict. He wouldn't mind a life of peace if he was able to share it with Kerry.

That wasn't to be of course so he had no option but to marry Nessa. He dressed and left the infirmary, the heat of the fire soon no more than a distant memory. If only he could say the same of Kerry.

Chapter Fourteen

❧❀❧

Kerry had made her mind up. She would
wait until they got to the old hall and
then cry out for help. The place had
been deserted when she'd last been there but
Callum had told her why. They had all been
summoned to the castle or something like that,
leaving the way clear for a MacCleod to enter
MacIntyre land without sparking war.

There were bound to be people there this time.
She might not be able to escape the painful grip
Edward had on her but she wouldn't need to.
Once they got there and she started screaming the
entire population would come charging over and
in the confusion she'd run for it. She'd get through
the portal on her own and keep running. In her

own time the police would be able to help her keep Edward away. Here she could only rely on herself.

There was no point trying to get to Callum. She would only make his life worse.

He had to marry Nessa. That was the conclusion she'd reached as they grew closer to MacIntyre hall. She kept looking around her for any sign of life but there was nothing yet.

She'd decided it would be better for him to marry the woman he was supposed to. Even if he did love Kerry it wouldn't be possible for the two of them to be together, not really. They were from different worlds. He was used to violence and death surrounding him but she wasn't. Not only that but if she stayed she risked causing clan war.

Edward would keep chasing her too and she shuddered to think of the damage he could do to a medieval people. What if he brought a gun back with him? Even the strongest medieval Highlander could do little against a revolver or a shotgun.

Or what if he tried some sports almanac shenanigans? The future might be President Edward. The idea didn't bear thinking about.

She would get through the portal and then she would destroy it. That was the only way to protect the past and the future. How could she destroy it? She would work that out when she got there.

The main thing she needed to do was break free from him. Could she get through the portal and destroy it before he got through? Could that work? Leave him stuck in the past to get an arrow through the throat when he picked on the wrong High-lander. That might just work.

She would be in the present and it would be as good as killing him but without any of the moral complications. He'd be trapped in the past and she'd finally be safe.

The downside would be that she would never get to be with Callum. She did her best not to think about that part.

They turned a corner and there was the hall in front of them. A plume of black smoke was rising from it. The hall itself was ablaze.

It was a hellish image and for a moment Kerry couldn't take in what was happening. There was too much to see.

Edward's hand slipped from hers as he stood in shock staring at the sight before him.

An old woman burst out from the flames, appearing in the doorway and then staggering away. At the same moment a group of men carrying flaming torches were running over to the hovels next to the hall. Another group of men on horseback were riding in from the road to the right.

"We need to help them," Kerry said, taking a step forward.

Edward blocked her way. "No we don't. We need to go home."

"But there are people in trouble." Already the men with torches were setting fire to the hovels, the thatch was alight, more dark smoke rising into the air. "They need our help."

"Don't you get it? These people are already dead. They died hundreds of years ago."

"No they didn't." She saw another person bursting out from the doorway, this one also somehow not ablaze. "They're alive right now."

"Listen, we're going home and that's all there is to it."

"How?"

"What?"

"How are we going home. The place is an inferno."

"She just came out of it and that guy just ran inside. It can't be that bad."

Glancing from side to side, Kerry thought about screaming but realized the noise would be lost against the roar of the fire. As she looked past the village she saw the old woman stagger back and vanish out of sight.

Edward had let go of her again and was busy staring at the fight. She took her chance, running as fast as she could toward the old woman. She heard him shouting behind her but she didn't look back, sprinting across the grass toward what she saw was a steep riverbank.

She stopped at the edge and looked down into the foaming torrent. There she was, her head just vanishing below the waves. "Hold on," she shouted, sliding her way down the bank, her arm outstretched. She tried to stop at the edge but the grass was slick with dew and she was unable to prevent herself from losing balance.

With a single gasp she fell headfirst into the river and was immediately lost under the water. Opening her eyes she saw the old woman floating nearby, the two of them being fast washed downstream. Putting on a spurt of speed she kicked her legs and grabbed hold of the stranger, lifting her head to the surface so she could breathe.

The current was too strong for her to do anything but hold onto the unconscious woman and pray they both made it out of the river alive.

She had no idea how long they floated through the churning torrent but after an eternity of fighting for breath and spitting out foam the current finally began to slow and she was able to look around her. On both sides were trees lining the bank. The smoke from the fire at the old hall was nowhere to be seen. The only sound was the river and her own labored breathing.

Rolling onto her back, she kicked with her legs, keeping her arm around the old woman who still hadn't moved. Eventually she made it to the bank, using the last of her strength to drag her companion onto the grass.

Utterly exhausted she laid back, her eyes closing at once. The sound of the river faded away.

The next thing she knew she was lying in a lumpy bed hearing someone say "She's alive. I know she is."

Opening her eyes, she said, "Who's alive?"

She was in some kind of large hall,

"My daughter," the old woman next to her said. "She's at MacIntyre hall."

"That's a coincidence," Kerry replied, sitting up and looking around her. Who was the woman next to her? She knew her from somewhere. "That's where I was headed. Where am I?"

"Crossraguel abbey apparently."

"How do you know that?"

"The abbot just left. Is it true that you dragged me out of the river?"

All of a sudden the memories came flooding back. "I remember. You fell in and I went in after you. It had gone for a moment but now I remember."

"What's your name?"

She knew that without having to think. She knew everything that had happened from falling out of the window in MacCleod castle to that moment. "Kerry Sutherland."

"Janet Dagless. Thank you, for getting me out of the river I mean."

"Don't mention it. Any idea how we got here?"

"I think one of the monks found us on his way to a grange."

"A grange?"

"Like a farm but run by the abbey monks instead of tenant farmers."

"Oh, I see. So we're in an abbey. Is that allowed, us being women and all?"

"I heard them talking about that very subject. They want to move us to the guesthouse when we're well enough."

"I feel fine now. How about you?"

"All I want to do is get back to MacIntyre hall and find my daughter."

"Your daughter. What did she look like?"

"Like me but younger and with fewer wrinkles."

"What was she wearing?"

Janet described perfectly the woman that Kerry had seen walking out of the inferno moments after her mother. "I saw her," she said when the older woman was done. "She came out right after you."

"So she's alive? Thank god. I have to go find her."

"Hold on. You're heading up to MacIntyre hall?"

"Right this minute."

"Then let me come with you. You look like you're struggling to walk."

"I'm fine." Janet climbed out of bed and staggered on her feet for a moment. "Which way's out?"

"Come on. We'll go together. Find your daughter and then get back to our own time."

"Our own time. What do you mean our own time?"

Kerry swung her legs out of the bed, testing her balance as she stood up. Nothing seemed broken though she felt as bruised as she had when she woke up in the middle ages for the first time. "Brace yourself for a bit of a shock but this isn't the twenty-first century."

"You're kidding, right?"

"I'm not. This is the twelfth century and we're in the middle of clan territory in the Highlands."

"Are you sure you didn't hit your head when you went underwater?"

"You'll see soon enough. Come on, let's get going. The sooner we head north, the sooner we get home."

As they made their way outside, Kerry thought fast. They needed to get to the old hall. That part should be easy enough. Edward might be hiding there though, waiting for her to come back. She would need to keep an eye out for him.

Once she was certain it was safe she would get the two of them through to the present, hopefully with Beth with them too. Then she would find a way to destroy the doorway so Edward couldn't follow them.

That was if the doorway was still there. What if the fire had destroyed it? She tried to think about how it had looked. It was made of stone. Wouldn't that give it a chance to survive the inferno?

Eventually she decided not to worry about it. There was nothing she could do but get there and find out for herself whether it still existed.

To do that they needed to get out of the abbey, not easy when the entire place seemed surrounded by a tall stone walls.

When they got near the church she heard the sound of male voices singing in unison, the sound echoing out toward them, loud in the quiet of the day.

"They must be in the middle of a service," she said. "Perfect timing for us to get out of here."

"How? There's a guard on the gate."

Kerry tried each door they came to. She found what she wanted on the third attempt. A pile of clothing waiting to be washed. "Put this on," she said to Janet before slipping a habit over her own clothes.

A few minutes later they were outside the walls and heading north, just two laborers walking from one job to another.

Chapter Fifteen

Callum had managed to find an hour to himself. The peace it brought him was in stark contrast to the chaos going on inside the castle. The wedding preparations were in full flow and everywhere he turned someone was asking him something.

He didn't care about whether the flowers would wilt if they were picked too early, nor what color they were. He didn't care about the amount of grain being brought out of the winter store to provide the feast. He didn't even care about his future bride.

He had tried. He had done his best to make conversation with her but she had made it abun-

dantly clear she wanted absolutely nothing to do
with him.

The very first time they'd met, she had whispered in his ear, "I want to make it very clear that I
have no desire to marry a MacCleod."

"Point taken," he replied, looking around the
great hall at all the happy diners. Everyone was
enjoying the meal apart from him.

"If I had my way I would marry the man I
love," she continued. "A man with MacKay blood
running through his veins."

"I get it."

"I hate you."

It was fair to say their initial encounter did not
go as well as Callum's parents might have hoped.

Standing next to the shore of the loch, the only
sound was that of the water gently lapping at the
heather covered grass. Across the water two curlews
were coming into land. The sun had not long risen
and streaks of orange and red coated the far moun-
tainsides. The tops were sprinkled with the first
snows of the winter. It would not be long before a
white blanket covered most of the MacCleod lands.

Mild autumns always led to severe winters.
Callum found himself thinking about the amount
of food in the castle stores, making rough calcula-

tions about how much was going to waste. First the feast to celebrate the betrothal and now more for the wedding feast. Would there be enough for the winter?

What he wanted to do was go back inside and call off this farce. She did not want to marry him. She had made clear there was a man she loved back at MacKay castle and if only she had an excuse to cancel the ceremony she would take it without a moment's hesitation.

He could give her an excuse. He could tell her about Kerry, tell her that he too was in love with another woman.

He had thought about raising the issue but decided against it. The wheels were in motion. The wedding was going to happen. If she backed out his father would likely banish him for all time.

Besides, he thought as he skimmed a stone across the water, he hadn't heard a thing from Kerry since she left. No doubt she was already back home in her own time. Would she look him up in her history books? Find out what had happened to him?

If she did she would see that he married Nessa MacKay like he was supposed to. There would be no mention of his inability to summon up any positive feelings about the wedding. How he'd watch her berating the kitchen girls for burning her toast, yelling at them until they cried. How she'd demanded, and been given, better accommodation at the castle, thicker blankets, a bigger bed, more servants. She seemed determined to make as many enemies as possible but no matter what she did, his parents turned a blind eye. Even when she kicked the farrier's cat from the battlements for hissing at her, Alan MacCleod just turned away and said nothing.

"Did you not see that?" Callum said to him. "You would still have me marry her?" The cat limped away, mewling piteously.

"You have to marry her to align the clans," his father replied through gritted teeth, walking away without another word.

Callum felt something by his ankle. Looking down he saw the bundle of fur purring and rubbing against his leg. "Good morning Roughshod," he said, reaching down to stroke the cat's head. "Glad to see your leg's on the mend."

The cat yawned loudly before darting its head to the left. Catching sight of a field mouse it stalked off leaving Callum to turn back to the loch. He felt more affection for Roughshod than he did for Nessa MacKay. She also didn't hiss at him as often.

A horn blew out in the castle, the sound echoing loudly around the valley. With a sigh Callum turned and headed back. The sound of his doom. Someone was looking for him. He doubted it would be anything good.

As he walked back up he thought about the men out on patrol. They had gone without him. He hadn't expected that. On the morning they were due to leave he had climbed out of bed before light and made his way to the stables only to find the horses were gone, the men were gone, and any hope he had of maintaining the life he desired was gone.

The Laird had sent them without him, insisted they go according to his mother despite their vocal protests. "It was patrol or be banished," she said to him when he found her in the solar. "They had no choice. You are soon to be wed. This is not the time to go out and get a sword to the gut."

On the way back up to the castle he kicked a stone as hard as he could. It struck the castle wall and bounced back with surprising force, catching him on the forehead.

"Violence often has unpredictable results," a voice said from the castle gates.

"Nice to have some sympathy," Callum replied, wiping the blood away from his eyes. "How are you Fingal?"

"Abbot Fingal now."

"Abbot? Which bunch of fools put you in charge?"

"The monks of Crossraguel have better judgment than you, Callum. In many things."

The abbot smiled, holding out a hand to shake. Callum took it, surprised by how strong the grip was. "It's good to see you."

"And you. What brings you here?"

"I came to bless the wedding."

"You've heard then?"

"All the Highlands have heard of the union of the MacCleods to the MacKays. The MacIntyres are thinking of uniting with the Campbells and the MacDonalds in return. They think you mean to invade."

Callum swore quietly. "The whole point of the wedding was to make things safer, to bring peace to the Highlands and Isles."

"Not everyone sees it that way. I tried telling your father but he will not listen. You marry Nessa and the other clans unite against you. All he sees is the dowry that will come with the wedding."

A light went on above Callum's head. "Of course. That's why he's not worried about wasting our food on the feast. He'll get the stores refilled by old man MacKay."

"And their people will starve instead."

Callum nodded. "Still, it must be done. I have no choice."

"Do you not?"

"What? Do you know something I dinnae?"

Fingal scratched his chin as he began to walk slowly into the castle, Callum by his side. "I had a woman brought into the abbey unconscious."

"I knew you monks were starved of female company but isn't that going a bit far?"

Fingal didn't laugh. "She mentioned a name in her sleep. In fact, she said the name many times."

"So what? What's that got to do with me?"

"It was your name, Callum MacCleod."

Callum stopped dead, grabbing Fingal by the arm. "Who was this woman? What did she look like?"

"Bruised and half drowned. She said her name was Kerry. Does that name mean something to you?"

"I must go to the abbey. I have to see her." He was already marching to the stable when Fingal stopped him. "What are you doing? Let go of me."

"She's no longer at the abbey."

"What? Why? Where did she go?"

"I've no idea but she left with another woman while we were in the middle of a service."

"But where have they gone?"

"I've no idea. I thought you might know. She is not well. Was muttering all kinds of things in her sleep about flying machines and boxes that can talk and all sorts of gibberish. Said she had to get back to the future like Marty McFly. I fear she is delirious. I have never heard of the McFly clan. Do you know of them?"

"No but I know she's not delirious." He smiled. "And I know where she's going.

"Where?"

"MacIntyre Hall. I just hope I'm not too late. Do me a favor."

"What?"

"Call off the wedding for me."

He ran for the stables without looking back. Two minutes later he was riding at full pelt out of the gate, ignoring the shouts of his parents who had appeared in the courtyard.

Spurring the horse on, he sped north. After an hour he looked behind him. No one was following.

That wasn't the case for long.

By the time he was halfway to MacIntyre hall he was convinced he was being followed. Whenever he looked back there were two horses, little more than dots at first but as time passed and his own steed began to tire they grew larger.

By late that evening he could make out two men riding as fast as they could to catch him.

He stopped only briefly at The Red Fox to change his horse before continuing on his way north, putting on a fresh burst of speed to outride the two men who had no doubt been sent after him from the castle.

If they thought they were bringing him back to marry Nessa they had another thing coming. They might be scouts of course, their job only to report on his whereabouts while a larger force was massed.

That got him thinking about MacIntyre hall. He was riding deep into MacIntyre territory and there was no good reason he could give if he were found there by a patrol. I am running from my wife to be and searching for a woman from the future. He could picture the laughter already.

Still, what could he do? He could stop and kill

them both but there were only two possible consequences of that. Clan war or his execution as a sop
to the MacIntyres.

Better to outride them. Find Kerry and
persuade her to stay. Nothing else mattered. It was
possible she was a liar but in his heart he knew that
wasn't true. He decided to trust his instincts. He
would find her and let the ancient spirits roll their
bones. How they landed was up to them. He could
only find her. The rest was up to fate.

Behind him the two riders drew near. Both of
them were wearing black suits that seemed very out
of place in the medieval Highlands.

Chapter Sixteen

⚜

Kerry lost sight of Janet in a wood a day's walk from MacIntyre hall. Rain was falling heavily and the last of the autumn leaves did little to keep it from soaking her.

She didn't realize they had become separated until it was too late. For some time they had been walking single file, slogging their way through the trees along a track which seemed to go on uphill forever. When she finally stopped and looked around her she could see nothing but darkness. The trail had become a muddy mixture of water and pine needles and it soaked through her shoes and froze her toes. Janet was nowhere to be seen.

Over the noise of the wind whistling through the branches she shouted for her companion but the only response was the trees creaking as they moved back and forth in the worsening storm.

Lost and alone she leaned back on a tree trunk and thought about her next move.

Closing her eyes she felt a strange sense of peace coming over her despite the icy chill of the wind. Her chattering teeth slowed and she was able to breathe again.

Let fate decide, she thought. She had no idea which way she was facing, let alone how far she had to go. She didn't remember the wood last time she was walking this way so she knew she was lost. There was no way of knowing for sure where MacIntyre hall was until it turned light. She could wait where she was or keep moving and see where she ended up.

Go home or go to him? While walking north with Janet from Crossraguel she had become increasingly unsure as to whether or not she was making the right decision. Go home and she risked bumping into Edward once again.

The peace that had filled her as she stood there in the wood remained as she thought of him. She felt stronger, as if he had become smaller, less of a threat. Perhaps she would just take a sword back with her and show him what she'd learned while she'd been here. Out of nowhere she felt as if she could easily defeat him in a sword fight. What was happening to her?

She didn't know it but she was standing in the exact spot that many centuries earlier had been home to a stone circle. Inside the stone circle a woman had blessed the stones, a woman who one day would walk along a pier on the English coast-line, a woman who owned a cat called Podgorny that stood beside her while she spoke to the spirits within the stones, talking to them of times past and future, how they were no more fixed in time than she was.

Kerry didn't know about any of that. All she knew was when she opened her eyes she knew exactly what to do. Walk out of the wood and head in a straight line. The rest was up to fate.

Standing still for a final moment, she felt the most immense connection with the land around her. Her feet seemed to reach into the soil as if she had become part of the landscape. She could feel the ground moving with the wind as if it were breath-ing. In the distance a hedgehog was settling down under a pile of leaves to hibernate. She could tell because she could feel its heartbeat.

It lasted only for the briefest of moments but

when it was gone she felt a wrenching sense of loss. In that moment she would have given anything to experience it again. She understood for the first time what Callum had been talking about when he told her about connecting to the land around him, being part of the Highlands. She felt it too.

She began to walk, feeling a strange sense of peace. She was on her own journey. It was one she had to take alone. She knew with absolute certainty that Janet was on her own journey. They might meet again. They might not. It didn't matter.

All that mattered was walking in a straight line and keeping going no matter how cold she felt. No matter how strong the wind became, no matter how heavy the rain, she would keep going until she reached her destination wherever it was.

The trees began to thin as the first light of gray dawn appeared in the distance. She paused, blinking in the rain, looking about her for a moment. The ocean was that way. In that direction was a range of mountains. How did she know that?

She shrugged and continued on her way. Over the course of the next hour the wind died down and the rain began to slow until by the time the morning had truly begun the clouds were slowly parting to allow a few rays of weak sunlight to shine through, lighting up the heather as if marking the way she was supposed to go.

In the distance she could make out a figure heading along a road, walking beside a donkey and cart. She reached the road a minute later, marching along it with a newfound sense of purpose.

As the figure grew nearer she could see a pile of turnips on the back of the cart. He nodded a greeting, tapping the donkey on the side. The grateful beast came to a stop, sniffing at the grass at its feet. "Good morrow," the man said, lifting his cap to scratch at his thinning black hair. "You look lost."

"Not lost," Kerry smiled. "I know exactly where I'm going. How about you?"

"Turnips to a wedding. Gift from the MacIntyres."

"Handing out turnips. How kind of them."

"A bit odd if you ask me."

"How so?"

He leaned toward her, glancing around him as if to check if anyone was listening. "Is it not a little strange handing out our food to the MacCleods? There's something fishy about this if you ask me."

"The MacCleods? Is it a MacCleod wedding?"

"How long have you been on the road for, I thought everyone knew."

"Knew what?"

"Young Callum MacCleod is marrying Nessa MacKay in a week's time. I'm to get these to their table before the ceremony and why? We have bones to pick with both clans." He shrugged. "But if I'm to keep my head on my shoulders I better get moving. Good day to you lass."

Kerry waved as he set off moving once more, the cart wheels creaking as they forced a way through the puddles on the road.

Fate had made the decision for her it seemed. She tried not to feel sad, wanting to keep hold of her recently acquired self confidence.

She didn't manage it. He was marrying someone else. She knew it was likely to happen of course but there had always been a tiny part of her that thought he might come back for her. It wasn't to be. She would just have to get used to living without him. She would have the memory of a single kiss and knowledge of a love so strong she would never feel it for anyone else for the rest of her life.

Some people never feel that, she told herself, starting to walk once more. She knew she should be grateful for the little time they had spent together but she couldn't stop thinking about the wedding.

He would stand opposite Nessa MacKay, smiling at her, their hands clasped together.

How different were wedding ceremonies back then? Would he put a ring on her finger? Recite vows? Go on honeymoon? The thought of it made her feel ill.

Steeling herself to keep moving she gritted her teeth. Fate had decided. If the cart was going to the wedding she was right to walk in the other direction. Any chance of happiness with Callum was long gone. All she could do was go home and try to be happy without him.

A tear fell from her eye but it was the only one she would allow herself. She had stamped on her emotions when she lived with Edward. She could do the same thing about Callum, shut down her feelings so she could continue to function.

What was that book? Feel the fear and do it anyway. She thought it needed a better title. Stamp on the fear so you can get on with it. Not as catchy but better fitting how she felt.

It was another day before she made it to the old hall. She had slept during the night in a tiny crumbling barn. It wasn't warm but it kept the wind out and allowed her to feel protected for at least a couple of hours. She found a couple of carrots that had been missed by the farmer, a miserly breakfast but at least enough to stave off her hunger until she made it home.

When the hall came into view she stopped. It was little more than a burned out shell. The fire had long since been extinguished. There was little left of the hovels standing beside it. Some rebuilding had taken place. Charred wood had been piled together to one side and fresh stone was in another pile. Whoever was working on it was nowhere to be seen when she arrived. The place was deserted, looking much as if it had been abandoned forever.

She walked over to the door, seeing down the cleared corridor to the bedroom. The stones that made up the doorframe at the far end of the corridor were still there. At least that was something. The portal should still work. A few more yards and she would be home. Best of all there was no sign of Edward anywhere.

She walked into the hallway and down toward the bedroom. There it was, the portal. On the other side was the future.

She didn't step through. She paused to think about everything that had happened to her since she arrived in the past. She had fallen in love and then lost him. Her ex had turned up and tried to force her to come home with him. She'd almost drowned. She had first hand knowledge of the medieval Highlands and how the people lived back then. She could become a historian, writing the most vividly realistic books about the middle ages.

A half smile crossed her lips but it faded almost at once. She put a hand onto the stone doorway, feeling it vibrating softly. She hoped Callum would find happiness even if it wasn't with her.

She took a step forward.

"Wait!"

The voice was so loud it sounded like it was right next to her. Who had said that?

Turning her head she looked out onto the grass. There was a man on the back of a horse. He was riding at full gallop toward her.

It was Callum.

She gasped, calling out his name. "Callum," and running back outside. She had barely made it when two more horses appeared from the river-bank. Had they been hiding there?

On their backs were two men in black suits, their outfits looking completely out of place in the medieval Highlands. They rode fast, getting between Callum and Kerry, riding full pelt toward her.

She screamed and ran, the two of them thundering after her, Callum close behind. She made it to the old hall, running into the hallway before skidding to a halt by the bedroom doorway.

"Go through," one of the men shouted, bringing his horse to a stop by the front door. "Do it."

"No," Callum shouted, climbing down from his horse and running after them as they chased her down on foot.

"Do it. Go through Kerry."

"How do you know who I am?" she asked, planting her feet squarely on the ground and refusing to move any further. "How do you know my name?"

Callum caught up with them, his sword held high. "Step aside."

"You can't do this," one of the men replied, holding out his hands to try and keep the two of them apart.

"The devil we can't," Callum said, swinging his sword menacingly through the air. "If you try to keep us apart a moment longer I will run you both through."

The older of the two men blanched. "Please,

don't kill us. Just turn around and go back to your home. That's the way things are meant to go."

Callum walked toward Kerry. The men were still in his way. He grabbed the nearer of the two, shoving him down to the ground. The man shrieked, landing with a thud.

Callum pressed his sword to the man's chest. "Talk."

"I told you," the man cried out, looking to his companion. "We shouldn't have gone after him. We were told not to interfere directly or we'd fail."

"Shut up," his older companion snapped. "What choice did we have? You want to go back and tell him it didn't work? You know what he'll do to us."

"Last chance," Callum said. "Talk. Who are you? Why have you been chasing me?"

The younger man looked up at the older one who just shrugged and said, "What does it matter now? You might as well tell him. We're both dead anyway."

"Talk!"

The younger man spoke fast, his eyes never moving from the tip of the sword. "Our employer needs you to marry Nessa like you're supposed to. That's all."

"Why? What does it matter who I marry?"

"Because you're supposed to marry her."

"Says who."

"Says history. If you marry Kerry you'll have children and…"

"And what?"

The older man took over. "And Alexander MacKay loses everything."

"Who's Alexander MacKay?" Kerry asked.

The old man sighed, rubbing the bridge of his nose with his hands. "We were hired to make sure Callum married Nessa. If he does, his wife hates him so much they never have children. The MacCleod line dies out and Alexander's ancestors invade, taking their land."

Kerry could hardly believe what she was hearing. "Why do I have to go through the doorway?"

"You weren't supposed to have so much free will. You were supposed to go back and stop causing problems. You're an outlying piece of datum, that's what you are and you should go home before you cause any more trouble."

"Watch it," Callum snapped. "You're talking about the woman I love.

"The younger man tried to stand but Callum held him fast with the sword.

"Keep talking," Kerry said. "What happens if the MacKays invade?"

"Fast forward to our time and Alexander owns half of Scotland. That's what's supposed to happen."

The older man leaned back against the doorway. "Then she goes and finds a portal to the past and it all goes wrong. You two get married, the MacCleods take over half the Highlands and help Robert the Bruce bring peace in a couple of centuries. In return he gives you more estates and the MacKays get nothing. Our job was to fix history so she didn't screw it up."

"How do you know all this?"

"Our employer was shown a second copy of The Saga of Callum MacCleod. It tells of what happens when Callum marries Nessa instead of Kerry. I know it sounds like a fairytale but I have seen the book. Look, please. You have to marry Nessa. It's the way history is meant to go."

"So the MacKays can rule Scotland and the MacCleod line can die out?"

The older man looked scared. "Please, try to see it from our point of view. If we go back and tell him you're staying with Kerry what will he do to us?"

"Why don't you find out?" Callum dropped his

sword, grabbing the two of them in his enormous arms and tossing them through the doorway. They vanished at once.

With an enormous grunt he shoved the lintel above the doorway. It creaked and began to shift. "Last chance," he said to Kerry. "Are you going or staying?"

"What do you think?" she replied, helping him to push the doorway over. The stones collapsed into a heap, dust rising into the air as they turned to face each other. "It's over," Callum said. "No going home."

"I am home," she replied, her hands slipping into his as the dust began to slowly settle once more.

He smiled, leaning down to kiss her. She closed her eyes. A moment later their lips touched and any doubts she had about making the right choice vanished, never to be thought about again.

His arms slipped around her and their bodies pressed together, their embrace continuing. Kerry thought of nothing at all but the feel of him against her. They had come so far together. She had thought she'd lost him forever and the joy she felt at his kiss was nothing to the joy of knowing he had come back for her.

"I love you," he said, pulling back long enough to stroke her hair, drinking in her image.

"I love you too," she replied, pulling him back toward her. "Kiss me again."

He did, many times. It was much later that they began their journey south together. They would never see MacIntyre hall again.

Chapter Seventeen

✿✿✿

E dward looked a mess. He hated the
middle ages. He hated Scotland. It was
nothing but mud and wind and rain and
there was nothing to look at. All he could see were
miserable mountains that contained no food, empty
fields that contained no food and no shops.

It had taken weeks to track down Kerry since
she so stupidly fell into the river. He finally heard a
rumor she was in an abbey and he got there in time
to find out she'd left. Would the monks give him a
meal and some clean clothes? Only if he joined
them in a service. Like that was ever going to
happen. Those god botherers weren't going to hook
him into their nonsense. They might believe in
fairies in the sky but not him. He laughed at their

suggested deal and headed back north to look for her, stealing food from anywhere he could manage to find it.

The last two days he hadn't eaten the thing. The last meal he'd had was a loaf of bread snatched out of the hand of a whining child in a village that was as muddy as he was. That meal had earned him a chase from a farmer with an ax and he'd barely gotten away.

The chase was meant to happen though because running from that brought him toward Kerry. He found her not long after finally losing his pursuer.

She was walking with the woman she'd pointed out at the old hall. Edward didn't know what they were doing together. What he did know was if he followed them long enough he should be able to get hold of her again. Then it would be a simple matter of going back through the portal and getting clean, scrape away the filth of this disgusting place and get back to normal. He might even make her wash him, the first step to paying him back for everything she'd put him through.

There would be a lot more pay back for all this, he thought as he tracked her and her companion. He was able to warm himself with thoughts of slapping her across the face, seeing the shocked look that always came when he taught her a lesson.

She couldn't be left alone, that much was obvious. Let go of her for one minute and she was off almost drowning. That wouldn't happen again, not on his watch. He'd keep a much closer eye on her when they got back. She'd be lucky if he ever let her out of the house again.

He followed the pair of them into a wood. The driving rain made it hard to keep track of where they were headed and by the time he was inside the treeline they'd vanished.

He did his best to find them, searching the wood until dawn but he saw nothing but his own footsteps.

He emerged the next morning with no idea where he was. He couldn't even tell which way he was heading. He would have killed for a compass.

Eventually he made it to the old hall. It seemed to have taken weeks but it was no more than a couple of days. There was no sign of her the entire journey but that didn't matter.

He had passed by some dumb farmer on an empty cart and found out from him where she was.

When he described Kerry the farmer smiled a

black toothed smile of recognition. "Rode south with Callum MacCleod not two days ago."

Edward kept the smile on his own face until he was far in front of the farmer. That was her game was it? Get back together with that Highland imbecile? Was she as thick as him?

Edward made his mind up as he walked. The plan was simple. Go back through the portal and get some nice modern weapon. The farmer had given him the idea. Get hold of a gun. Come back. Kill Callum. Take Kerry home with him where she belonged.

It was a simple plan but there was one flaw to it. A flaw he only discovered when he reached the hall.

Someone had knocked the doorway down. He tried piling the stones back up but when he walked through nothing happened. The magic, whatever it had been, was gone.

He lost it. Something inside his mind snapped. He couldn't get back to the future and it was all their fault.

He headed south once more. Encrusted with filth he muttered to himself as he went. "Stuck here in the middle ages. No soap. No showers. No TV. No car. Freezing cold and filthy and it's all their fault. No way back. They're laughing at me right now. I bet they're having great chucks about old Edward. Well, they won't be laughing when I catch up with them. Let them laugh. See how that Scots prick laughs with a knife in his back. And her? She'll get me clean and maybe I'll run his stupid clan for a while, make her my wife. I might not be able to get back but I can make them pay for keeping me here. They'll pay all right. They'll both pay."

He continued ranting as he walked. Anyone who saw him gave him a wide berth. They recognized madness when they saw it.

He kept walking, knowing he would get to MacCleod castle soon enough. And he did.

When he saw it he knew at once he was there. He could feel the two of them in there. He could almost hear them pointing and laughing at him as he approached.

If the guards had been paying attention he would never have made it inside. They were too busy with the wedding preparations to notice what he did.

Edward watched them from behind a tree. He waited until a cart rolled past covered in rushes. With a single leap he buried himself inside the rushes, breathing in their warmth, feeling heat return to his limbs for the first time in days.

He listened as they continued arguing with a man who wanted paying up front for his eggs. While the argument continued the cart was able to roll straight past and then he was in the courtyard.

Sliding out from his hiding place he looked about him. He wouldn't have long before someone noticed him. He needed to move fast. Where would they be?

He went to the kitchen first. The cook noticed him and yelled at him to leave, chasing him out of the door. Hiding behind an archery target he watched the cook talking to one of the guards, no doubt looking for him. They wouldn't find him until it was too late. He only needed a minute. It wouldn't take long to do what he planned.

"Get me stuck here in this hellhole," he muttered as he emerged from behind the target and made his way over to the keep. They were bound to be in there.

The place was busy which played in his favor. No one noticed as he looked in one room and then the next, all the time fingering the knife in his back pocket. Maybe he'd mark her with his initials. Let all these bumpkins know she belonged to him, not their idiotic Laird.

He found her in the tower. A memory came back to him as he climbed the spiral staircase. He'd been here before. Then he remembered. This was where she'd fallen out of the window and all his problems had begun. This was all her fault. He was cold, tired, and filthy and it was all because she wouldn't listen to him, wouldn't come home like she was supposed to, wouldn't do as she was told.

He pulled the knife out as he climbed. He could hear her humming to herself. She sounded happy. She wouldn't be happy for long, not until she'd apologized for everything she'd put him through. He'd teach her a lesson and then he'd go find that Scotch prick and run him through for looking at his bird.

He couldn't wait to see the look on Callum's face when he realized he'd been bettered by Edward.

Later, he told himself. First, deal with her. He walked up the last few steps and pushed open the door, stepping into the tower room. "Here we are again," he said, gratified to see her yelp with shock at his sudden appearance.

"Edward?" she asked, squinting. "Is that you?"

"Of course it's me," he snapped, wiping mud from his face before taking a slow step toward her. "Don't you even recognize your own partner?"

"You're not my partner. We broke up."

She didn't look scared of him. That was irritating. He held the knife out in from of him, waving it slowly from side to side. Still she didn't look afraid. Why not? Was she too stupid to realize she was about to be taught a lesson she'd never forget?

"You can't marry Callum," Edward said, stopping in the middle of the room. "You belong to me."

"No, I don't," she replied, her arms by her side. "Look at you, Edward. You're a mess."

"I'm a mess because you went and threw yourself in a river and I had to go through hell tracking you down. Now, come and sit down. It's time for your lesson."

"No, Edward. I'm done with you and your lessons. Now why don't you just turn around and leave?"

He barked out a laugh. "Leave? You want me to leave after everything I've done for you?"

"What have you done for me? You've made me afraid to be myself but not anymore. You've broken my ribs. I nearly lost an eye because of you but you know what? I'm done with being scared of you. You want to come at me with that knife you go for it but you better make it good because you're only getting one shot."

Edward roared with anger. "You will be scared of me!" He lunged forward, swiping the knife down through the air, aiming to cut her face just enough to see that fear in her eyes that he so loved to see.

She still refused to look scared. He lost control, screaming and running at her as she darted backward. He lunged with the knife and as he did so he over reached, losing his balance and falling.

He wasn't worried. She would catch him. She wouldn't dare let him hurt himself.

She stepped to the side and he had time to see the sky outside the window before he fell through it, unable to stop himself in time.

He turned over in the air, looking back up and seeing the tower above him as he fell. She didn't even look out at him. He was furious. He would make her pay for this. He'd do more than just teach her a lesson. He would hurt her so much she-

His body thumped into the ground, the knife falling from his hand and running down the side of the moat, sinking into the water.

Hundreds of years later a metal detectorist

would dig up the knife and get it dated. When he was told it was only ten years old he would throw it out. He had bet it was older from how corroded it was but he lost the bet. He had no idea a knife bought in 2008 had been in the moat for centuries.

Edward didn't know anything about what happened to his knife. He lay perfectly still not knowing anything at all.

Chapter Eighteen

Callum stood on the battlement overlooking the front gate of the castle. There was no one left outside. All the guests were already crammed into the great hall. He looked out at the countryside, every lump and bump of the landscape as familiar to him as his own hand.

It felt strange to think that the next time he stood up there he would be a married man. He would be a husband. He would have a wife.

He found himself thinking just how lucky he was. He had come back to MacCleod castle ready for a blazing row with his parents. He took Kerry with him into the great hall, finding his father on the dais dealing with petitioners and his mother reading by the fireside.

It was a source of great pride to him that both his parents could read and that they had taught him the difficult skill while he was still a child. His mother looked up from her book, smiling when she saw him.

"We were hoping you'd come back," she said. "The abbot said you went north. I feared you went to pick a fight with the MacIntyres. Were you that desperate to get out of your wedding that you would get yourself killed in a pointless skirmish?"

"I went to fetch someone."

"Hi," Kerry said, waving next to him. "Nice to see you again."

"You're back," Alan shouted from the dais. "Get over here. I want a word with you." He waved the petitioners away. "Everyone out but my son."

Kerry looked unsure but Callum slipped his hand into hers, bringing her forward with him. The room emptied as he stood before his father, ready for the yelling to begin. "I will not marry Nessa MacKay," he said, bracing himself for the response.

"Aye," his father replied. "I know that."

"What?" Callum was thrown. "You are not angry with me?"

"Why would I be angry with you?"

"Because you've insisted on this wedding for weeks and told me if I didnae go through with it, I'd be banished."

"Aye well I didnae expect Nessa to run off in the night and marry her man before anyone could stop her, did I?"

"She ran off?"

"Said she'd be damned before she'd marry a MacCleod. So that's that."

Callum turned and smiled at Kerry. "Which means there's nothing to stop us marrying."

"Only one thing," she replied.

"What's that?"

"You haven't asked me yet."

Callum leaned over the battlements, recalling how she looked in that moment, the sparkle in her eyes, the amused look, the way the light from the fire made her hair glow with life. She looked more beautiful than ever as he asked her the only question that mattered.

"Will you marry me?"

"Of course I will."

"That's good news," Alan said, slapping their hands together. "I would have hated to see all that food go to waste."

"Is the alliance threatened?" Callum asked.

"Old man MacKay is so embarrassed by his daughter's actions that he gladly signed a peace treaty just to sweep it all under the rug."

Gillian got up from her fireside chair and walked over, looking closely at Kerry. "You love him, don't you?" she asked.

"I do," Kerry replied. "With all my heart."

"Then you have my blessing."

He smiled as he turned from the battlement and descended the stairs to the courtyard. He was lucky for many reasons. The bitter rivalry with the MacKays was at least temporarily abated. He had met a woman who'd traveled across centuries to be with him, a beautiful, a woman who was waiting for him in the chapel at that very moment.

He was lucky that Edward hadn't snatched her away from him. He was lucky that she was so fast on her feet that Edward had fallen out of the tower window when he had managed to sneak into the castle to attack her. He was lucky that she hadn't returned to the future. He was lucky she had decided to stay.

He smiled as he pushed open the doors of the chapel and walked inside. Abbot Fingal was standing by the altar. Beside him Kerry was standing in a stunningly beautiful tartan dress. The MacCleod colors suited her. Behind her stood his parents, both of them in their finest attire.

The chapel was crammed with people. Everyone but the guards on duty had squeezed in. They all watched Callum as he walked in, moving aside to allow him to pass through the crowd.

"Glad you decided to join us," Alan whispered as Callum passed him. "It's bloody freezing in here and your bride to be is turning into an icicle waiting for you."

"He's on time," Gillian hissed. "You kept me waiting for over an hour, remember."

Alan colored as Callum walked by to stand beside Kerry.

The abbot smiled at them both, clearing his throat before beginning. "We are gathered here today in the sight of God and the MacCleod clan to witness the blessed union of two people dear in the hearts of many. Kerry, since your arrival I hear tell you have revolutionized the way meals are prepared in the castle kitchen."

"I only showed them how to prep a few things," she replied.

"It was a lot more than that," someone shouted from the back. Callum turned to see one of the cooks step forward. "She's taught me how to make scones, sponge cake, Norman toast, jam tarts. I never knew of such things until she came along. God bless that woman."

"If I might continue," the abbot said. "Kerry, you have brought joy to many but you brought the most joy to Callum MacCleod, son of Alan and Gillian who both give their consent for this union today. Callum, you have protected the clan for years with your men."

"Aye," said a chorus of gruff voices at the back of the chapel, one of them adding, "When he's not off chasing women or drinking ale."

A ripple of laughter went around the chapel.

The abbot ignored them. "If you two are to wed today know this. You become part of the Highlands. You marry not just each other but also God and Scotland. If you agree to this, say aye."

"Aye," they said in unison.

"Callum, will you take this woman to be your wife, to protect and to worship, to take care of for the rest of your lives, to love and cherish until the day you die?"

"I will."

"Kerry, will you take this Highland fool for your husband, to protect and to worship, to take care of for the rest of your lives, to love and cherish until the day you die?"

"I will."

"Do you have the rings that show all here present that you are true to your vows?"

Alan and Gillian held out their hands, palms upward, two gold rings waiting to be taken.

Callum took his first, sliding it onto Kerry's finger, looking at her all the while.

Kerry lifted hers from Gillian's hand, looking at it in wonder and smiling as she placed it onto Callum's finger.

"You are now wed in the eyes of God and man and the Highlands themselves," the abbot said. "Go forth from this place as husband and wife and gather heather under the gate with my blessing."

The crowd streamed out of the church, Callum and Kerry last to leave as tradition dictated. They made their way hand in hand to the gate where a sprig of heather had been placed on a slab of wood on the ground. Callum lifted the heather into the air, showing it to the crowd before attaching it to Kerry's dress with a silver pin. With that done the crowd cheered and as they did so he leaned forward, kissing his wife for the very first time.

The feast came next. Everyone in the local villages had provided something and the tables sagged with the weight of it all. There was no space to move in the great hall, everyone talking and laughing, indulging in what might be the last large meal before the winter. Rumor was it that snow was coming and soon all would be hunkered down to ride out the cold months.

The thought of winter was far from anyone's thoughts while they ate, cheering the happy couple who sat together on the dais, surrounded by well-wishers.

"Are you happy?" Callum asked, seeing Kerry examining the ring on her finger. "Not having second thoughts?"

"I couldn't be happier," she replied. "This is where I was always supposed to be. I know that now. What about you? Wouldn't you rather have married Nessa?"

"I would rather have wed a sheep than her."

"So you're calling me a sheep?"

"No, that's not what I…" He smiled. "You're teasing me, aren't you?"

"Maybe." She winked and blew him a kiss as a horn echoed around the room.

The talking died down as Alan stood up, his

tankard held high in the air. "I wish to read you a poem."

Callum frowned. His father had never shown any interest in poetry.

"It was told to me by my father on my wedding day and today I hand it to my son who may one day pass it to his." He cleared his throat, his voice becoming quieter.

"Our land we bought with blood violent spilt,

Many have died to stitch the MacCleod quilt,

We remember them now and shall never forget,

All they've done for our clan and yet,

Today we look beyond all that is gone and past,

To the future of these two and may their love last,

Until the end of time when the last star doth fall,

So please raise a glass in cheer one and all."

An earsplitting roar went up around the room and Alan turned to Callum. "To my son and his wife, may they grant me a grandson to add one more panel to the MacCleod quilt."

"I have something to say."

The room fell quiet. At the furthest table a figure was rising. It was Moira. She had not been seen since Orm's funeral and was still wearing the clothes of mourning. In her arms she held a tiny sleeping baby.

She looked straight at Callum as she continued. "If Orm were here today he would have something to say but I must say it on his behalf." She paused, a tear rolling down her cheek. "May God bless your marriage as He once blessed mine." She sat down again without another word, rocking the baby slowly from side to side.

The feast continued long into the night. Outside snow began to silently fall, coating the castle and the land beyond in a blanket of white. The thick flakes hissed when they landed on the torches that illuminated the courtyard.

Eventually the door to the great hall opened and Callum emerged with his new bride. Behind them the abbot walked slowly, muttering his prayers. The door was pulled closed once more to keep the heat in as the three of them walked up the stairs to the bedchamber. The noise died away as they climbed. Kerry paused at an arrow slit to look outside at the falling snow. "It's beautiful," she said.

"Aye," Callum replied, kissing her cheek, "though nowhere near as beautiful as you."

Epilogue

K erry knelt before the small altar in the bedroom. Beside her Callum was muttering a prayer. The abbot stood behind them both.

The day had passed by in a blur. This was the first moment of quiet she'd had to contemplate everything that had happened. She was married. With this final prayer the elaborate wedding ceremony was completed and the abbot would bless their bed before leaving the two of them alone.

They were married. So much had happened since she had first met Callum that she found it hard to believe it had really happened. Part of her thought it might be the cruelest of dreams, that she would wake up back home and all of this would vanish.

She pinched herself discreetly. Nothing happened except her arm hurt. The abbot tapped her on the shoulder. Callum had finished.

The two of them stood up, the abbot smiling as he bowed to the altar before turning to them.

"Forgiveness is a true virtue," he said. "That you could forgive Edward for what he did to you is astonishing."

"I forgave him for me, not for him. I will never let him have power over me again."

"You're a better person than me," Callum said. "I still can't believe he tried to kill you."

"He remembers nothing of that," the abbot replied. "He spends his time in the infirmary hearing tales of the MacCleods who are a source of great wonder to him."

"His memory has not returned then?"

The abbot shook his head. "He believes he has always lived at the abbey. He knows only that he cannot walk and never will again."

"What does he do at the abbey?"

"He has been writing a saga. I bring you a copy he made himself."

He handed over a pile of parchment bound

inside leather. Kerry opened it and looked at the title. The Saga of Callum MacCleod.

"Edward wrote this?" she said, flicking through the pages. "I can hardly believe it."

"He is working on the second volume as we speak."

"I am glad the fall didn't kill him," she said to Callum. "Or I would never have read this book nor known anything about you." She meant it too. She wanted Edward out of her life but she wasn't sure she would have been able to handle having his death on her conscience.

She had been as surprised as anyone to find out Edward had awoken with no memory of the future or her. He thought he'd been born in the middle ages and accepted his lot at the abbey without argument. By all accounts he was a different person to the man who had tried to attack her in the tower, convinced he'd lived in the Highlands all his life. He even had a Scottish accent.

"I will leave you with one piece of advice," the abbot said, pressing the couple's hands together. "Your bond is the strongest I have ever seen between two people. I hope you can create a bond as strong with the other clans of the Highlands in defense of our lands. A good night to you both."

He turned without another word, heading out of the door and closing it behind him.

Kerry sank into a chair, exhaling heavily. "Alone at last."

"Aye," Callum replied. "So we are." He put a hand on her shoulder, squeezing lightly while looking into the fire. "How does it feel to be married?"

"It feels right."

He lifted her to her feet, wrapping his arms around her. "I love you Kerry MacCleod."

"I love you Callum MacCleod." Together they moved over to the bed and he began to undo the knot tying the shoulder of her dress. "One thing you need to know," she added, slapping his hand away.

"What's that?"

"Tonight you don't get to say we must wait until we're married to do this."

Her dress was thrown to the floor a moment later followed by Callum's tartan soon after.

The candles burned lower until they spluttered and went out leaving the room in darkness. The fire turned to embers, the temperature dropping rapidly.

In the bed, behind the heavy curtains, Callum

and Kerry wore nothing at all and yet they remained as warm as it was possible to be.

The End

Made in the USA
Monee, IL
28 May 2021